Andrew Buchanan

The Forces Which Carry on the Circulation of the Blood

Andrew Buchanan

The Forces Which Carry on the Circulation of the Blood

ISBN/EAN: 9783337394097

Printed in Europe, USA, Canada, Australia, Japan

Cover: Foto ©Andreas Hilbeck / pixelio.de

More available books at **www.hansebooks.com**

THE FORCES

WHICH CARRY ON THE

CIRCULATION OF THE BLOOD

BY

ANDREW BUCHANAN, M.D.

PROFESSOR OF PHYSIOLOGY IN THE UNIVERSITY OF GLASGOW

SECOND EDITION

LONDON

J. & A. CHURCHILL, NEW BURLINGTON STREET

1874

TO

THE VERY REVEREND PRINCIPAL

AND

THE PROFESSORS

OF THE

UNIVERSITY OF GLASGOW

DEAR SIRS,

Permit me to offer to you the homage of these pages. I do it with much respect, and with a full sense of the honour thereby reflected on myself. Next to loyalty to my Queen and country there is no feeling in my bosom more strong than loyalty to the Senate of the University of Glasgow. To become a member of that august body was the fond dream of my youth, and satisfied the highest ambition of my maturer years. It has been to me during a long lifetime the source of great and very pure happiness, cherishing, as I have always done, towards all of my colleagues in office feelings of genuine fraternal regard, and towards the Senate itself sentiments of the most profound respect and unfeigned admiration.

Believe me to be,

Dear Sirs,

With much regard,

Yours sincerely and devotedly,

ANDREW BUCHANAN.

4 ATHOLL PLACE, GLASGOW;
14th October, 1874.

TABLE OF CONTENTS

PART I

THE FORCE OF THE HEART, EFFECTIVE AND ABSOLUTE

PART II

THE VASCULAR FORCES

PART III

THE PNEUMATIC FORCES

THE FORCES

CIRCULATION OF THE BLOOD

PART I

THE FORCE OF THE HEART, EFFECTIVE AND ABSOLUTE

BORELLI estimated the force of the heart at 180,000 lb.,
Tabor at 150 lb., Hales at 51 lb., Jurin at 15 lb., and Kiel
at 5 oz. These discordant estimates formed by men of emi-
nence brought discredit on mathematical reasoning, as applied
to explain the action of living organs. The attempt to determine the mechanical force of the heart has ever since been
tacitly abandoned by most physiologists, who have regarded it
as a problem which there was more wisdom in passing over
than in attempting to resolve. Thus Magendie, after pointing
out the extreme estimates of Kiel and Borelli given above, contents himself with exclaiming "Where shall we find the truth
amid such contradictions?" This is tantamount to declaring
the problem to be beyond the reach of the human faculties.
Nothing, however, can be more inconsistent with the views
which are entertained at the present day as to the fundamental principles of physiology, the true nature of which
Magendie himself had so large a share in establishing.*
Physics and Chemistry are now regarded as the foundation of
physiology, except in so far as it rests upon Psychology. But if

---

* 'Phenomènes Physiques de la Vie,' par M. Magendie. Paris, 1842.

1

the most recondite principles of the two former sciences are without hesitation referred to in the explanation of physiological phenomena, surely the most simple of all physical principles, the principles of Mechanics, cannot be regarded as having no legitimate place in physiological discussions. Neither is it true that there is a greater discrepancy of opinion in the mechanical than in many other departments of Physiology. It is simply, that in the former department an inexorable system of reasoning makes the slightest discrepancy conspicuous; every principle assumed, and every argument founded on it, having a precise value assigned to it, and the conclusions being rigorously deduced from the premises; while in too many of the other departments, such discrepancies are lost sight of amid vague generalities, ill-weighed arguments, and unwarranted conclusions.

It cannot therefore be reasonably maintained that the labour and ingenuity bestowed by the physiologists of the last century in measuring the force of the heart have been expended in vain; and that it is no duty of the physiologists of the present day to recognise gratefully, and form a fair estimate of those labours, while they join their own efforts to those of their predecessors to attain the end in view; never, however, forgetting that the task is one of ascertained difficulty; that much caution and circumspection are necessary in applying the simple principles of Mechanics to the complex actions of living organs; and that to presume to differ from Harvey, or Hales, or Borelli is to contend on their own field with the giants and demigods of a bygone age.

A single preliminary remark may be useful with respect to the mode of reasoning adopted when we apply mathematical principles to Physiology. As all physiological phenomena vary according to age, sex, and constitution; and many of them also in each individual, according to various contingent circumstances, influencing at different periods both body and mind; it may at first sight appear impossible to reason accurately with respect to them. Now it is quite true that the reasoning never can apply accurately to every case, nor to any one case at all seasons; but it may, nevertheless, represent quite accurately what occurs in them all within certain limits. This is done by means of average numbers. But when we reason from average and not from absolute numbers, the ultimate conclusion applies only in any individual case according as the average numbers assumed correspond more or less exactly with the actual numbers in the case referred to. The average numbers are worthy of complete reliance when they are deduced from a large number of exact observations. Such in every society where accurate records of births and deaths are kept are the mortuary numbers applicable to the whole community, or to persons of either sex, or of whatever age; such numbers having been shown by experience to form a secure basis for the vast pecuniary transactions contingent on the duration of human life. But such numbers cannot be obtained with respect to many physiological phenomena which do not admit of being subjected to exact observations. In all such cases much judgment is requisite to select numbers which are certainly within the range of what actually occurs, and probably not far from the true average; and as minute accuracy is unattainable, a simple number forming a convenient coefficient in the computations into which it enters, is to be preferred to a complex number of doubtful certainty. Thus the duration of the systole of the heart was held by the physiologists of last century to be one third of the period from one pulse to another, or of a complete cardiac revolution. Some modern physiologists, aided by the increased facility of observation which the stethoscope supplies, have preferred the proportion of two fifths of the whole period, which is just one fifteenth longer than one third. As the difference is very minute, when the whole period is no more than five sixths of a second; and as it is impossible to have much reliance on the observations by which so minute a difference is established, either proportion may be taken—the former having the preference for the most part when the number of the pulse is not defined; but the latter being sometimes preferable, as for instance, in giving the time of the systole at exactly one third of a second, when the pulse is seventy-two.

We have now first of all to explain the objects to which our present inquiry is to be directed.   To estimate the force of the heart appears at first sight to be a single problem which can admit of only one satisfactory solution.   But the force of the heart is an ambiguous expression, and has been employed by different authors in totally different senses which correspond to problems equally distinct.   These problems require to be resolved on different principles, and the results cannot possibly agree.   This is, indeed, the principal cause of the discrepancy pointed out above in the results obtained by the eminent men there mentioned, and when so considered that discrepancy redounds to their credit, and can never fairly be made a subject of obloquy to physiologists.

In illustration of this view I shall point out three different senses in which the words "force of the heart" have been employed by Borelli, by Hales, and by Kiel, and the three corresponding and totally distinct problems which they have endeavoured to resolve.

Borelli seeks to determine the absolute force of the heart, or sum of the forces which the whole muscular fibres of the heart, including both auricles and ventricles, actually put forth during the period of their contraction.   To do this he simply weighs the organ and compares the weight with that of other muscles of which he had previously determined the force.   This is the most comprehensive question that can be proposed, and when rightly answered must give the highest numerical result.

The second problem is that investigated by Hales and more recently brought prominently forward by the late Dr Arnott. It is to determine the absolute force of the left ventricle of the heart considered as a muscular organ—not, therefore, the sum total of the forces of the individual fibres of the ventricle, but the resultant of the forces of those fibres as combined and operating together in the mechanism of the heart.   Hales estimates the force of the ventricle at 51 lb., Dr Arnott at 60 lb.   These results are startling by their magnitude.   They all approach to or exceed half a hundredweight—a weight which would crush the heart beneath it and extinguish all power of motion.   It is impossible not to suspect some fallacy in the process of reasoning by which such extreme estimates have been deduced. But they have, nevertheless, been received universally ever since by all those who could neither refuse their assent to the experiments of Hales nor deny the validity of his arguments.

The third problem is that of Kiel, which I have on a former occasion enunciated to be, to determine the effective force of the heart in carrying on the circulation of the blood, or in other words to determine the work done by the heart, which is manifestly a problem totally different from the two former. It is in this sense solely, as corresponding to the problem just stated, that I employ the very convenient term *effective force* of the heart, which cannot be confounded with the term *absolute force* employed in either of the two significations indicated above.

The estimates of the effective force of the heart made by Kiel, by the Rev. Dr Haughton, and by myself are very moderate in amount compared with the absolute forces just mentioned; the former being expressed in ounces and the latter in pounds. But they agree remarkably with each other; the numerical differences being easily explained. Kiel's estimate is too low, because he has greatly under-estimated the largest element in the calculation, viz., the resistances opposed to the heart's action. In a letter inserted in the 'Lancet,' November 12th, 1870, and now reprinted in Appendix, I pointed out the coincidence of Dr Haughton's results and my own, and the different methods by which they were obtained. It is highly gratifying to me to find my own results so nearly in accordance with those of a man who has contributed so largely to advance our knowledge of the mechanical actions of the human body.

We are, then, to confine our attention to the two last of the problems indicated above, and commence with the last. To calculate the effective force of the heart we must know beforehand the mass of blood to be moved, the velocity with which it moves, and the obstacles which oppose its progress. More particularly we must know—1st. In what quantity, and with what velocity, the blood issues from the left ventricle of the heart: 2nd. What is the amount of the resistances or obstacles which oppose the movement of the blood; and possibly, also,

3rd. Whether there are any auxiliary forces which assist in overcoming those obstacles and propelling the blood; but we shall see that this last consideration may be omitted by a peculiar mode of treating the problem.

The velocity with which the blood issues from the heart could be at once determined if we knew the exact quantity of blood which the left ventricle discharges at each contraction, the number of contractions in a given time, and the size of the primary sectional area of the blood-vessels,* that is, the sum of the areas of the ascending aorta and of the two coronary arteries; for whatever length of an aortic tube of the same area the blood discharged in any given time, as in a minute, would exactly fill, the same is the measure of the velocity of the blood in a minute, or the space which the blood would pass over if it continued its motion for a minute with the same velocity with which it issued from the heart; the tube being always full, and being, although contractile, on the average of the size assigned to it.

The average arterial pulse, which is the same as the number of contractions of the heart per minute, is usually estimated at 72; and the primary sectional area of the blood-vessels has been very generally taken, according to Kiel's measurement, as ·4187 of a square inch. The range of the probable estimates that have been made of the quantity of blood emitted at each contraction, by the left ventricle of the heart in an adult, is from 1 to 4 oz. I assume 2 oz., the estimate of Harvey, as certainly within the limits of what actually occurs, and probably not far from the average. Combining these elements, we have 144 oz. of blood per minute expelled from the left ventricle of the heart. Now, 144 oz. of blood are in volume 237·6641 cubic inches, and would fill of a tube ·4187 square inch in area, a length of 47·30195 feet. This therefore is the velocity per minute of the blood issuing from the heart. The estimate of Kiel is 52 feet

---

* I have to acknowledge the kindness and friendly criticism of Dr Herbert Davies in pointing out to me an error into which I had fallen by under-estimating the size of the cardiac orifice of the aorta, and supposing it the same as the primary sectional area of the blood-vessels. In the present edition the latter expression, or one equivalent, is everywhere substituted for the former.

per minute, and that of Hales is 49¾. I assume, therefore, 50 feet per minute, or 10 inches per second, as a convenient number, certainly within the limits of truth, to denote the velocity of the blood as it issues from the left ventricle of the heart.

We have experimental evidence in confirmation of these estimates. The researches of Hering made by injecting chemical substances, easy of detection, into the blood-vessels of living animals, and noting the time when they could be detected in blood drawn afterwards, at distant parts of the sanguiferous circuit, show at least that the assumed velocity is not too high; while the experiments of Volkmann and of Vierordt, made with instruments fitted to measure directly the velocity of the current of blood, show that in the carotid of the dog the blood moves very nearly at the rate indicated above.

The second element which requires to be taken into account in estimating the force of the heart is the obstacles which the blood meets with as it passes along the sanguiferous circuit. After raising the aortic valves, it passes along a series of elastic tubes diverging from each other at various angles, gradually diminishing in size, and becoming more tortuous in their course as they diminish, till it arrives at the capillary system of vessels destined for the nourishment of the various tissues of the body, where it has to force its way through a network of canals so minute that in many of them not more than a single blood-corpuscle can pass at a time. From these canals the blood passes into the veins—a more capacious and distensible system of vessels, which bring it back to the heart. From this brief description it is easy to perceive the nature and magnitude of the obstacles which oppose the progress of the blood. It is useless to attempt to analyse them more minutely, as we are altogether unable to estimate the effect of any one of them, much less to determine in that way their total amount. The problem might, therefore, have remained long insoluble but for the ingenious experiments of the Rev. Mr. Hales,* who has taught us how to estimate the total amount of the resistances to

* " Hæmastaticks," being vol. ii of ' Statical Essays,' by Stephen Hales, B.D., F.R.S. London, 1738.

the movement of the blood as it issues from the heart, without reference to any of them singly. This method, also, is attended with a still further simplification, inasmuch as it enables us to dispense with all consideration of the auxiliary forces that promote the circulation of the blood. The only two notable auxiliary forces which we recognise below act, one of them in augmenting the resistance, the other in signally diminishing it; but without specifying either, the effect of both is taken into account in the experimental results of Hales.

The well-known experiments of Hales were made by inserting a tube into the carotid or crural arteries of various animals —the horse, the doe, the sheep, and the dog; and noting the height to which the blood rose in the tube, from the tension of the blood-vessels. He found in the horse the height of the column of blood to be from 8 feet 3 inches to 9 feet 8 inches; in the sheep, 6 feet 5¼ inches; and in 20 different dogs it was generally 5 feet. He therefore assumes 7½ feet, or 90 inches, a mean number between those just stated, as the height to which the column of blood would rise in the human arteries. As frequent reference will be made hereafter to this column, I shall speak of it, for the sake of brevity, as the "hæmastatic column" of Hales. The more recent experiments of Poiseuille confirm remarkably the results obtained by Hales. He has also shown that the height of the column of blood is the same in all the large arteries of the body.

It is only with the height of the column of blood in the arteries that we have at present to do; but as the height of the column in the veins has an important bearing on the second part of our subject, I subjoin a Table, gleaned from the work of Hales, exhibiting the relative heights of the hæmastatic column in the arteries and the jugular vein of different animals, and showing that the latter is just one tenth of the former.

	CAROTID. Inches.	JUGULAR. Inches.
Horse	100	12
Sheep	75	5·5
Dog	60	6
	235	23·5
Man . .	90	9

To apply the experiments of Hales to determine the amount of the obstacles which oppose themselves to the force of the left ventricle of the heart.

The semilunar valves at the root of the aorta are kept fast shut by the weight of a column of blood 90 inches in height, and ·4187 of a square inch in area; which is equal to

$$\underset{\text{Grains.}}{9,989\cdot 0370} = \underset{\text{Oz.}}{22\tfrac{3}{4}} + \underset{\text{Grains.}}{35\cdot 8815}$$

Suppose then a glass tube to be constructed of the form of the letter U, and ·4187 of an inch in area, one of the arms of the tube (A, Fig. 1) being 90 inches in height, while the other, H, is more than an inch higher; and let a valve opening, from H to A, be placed in the middle of the transverse part of the tube. If now the branch of the tube, A, be filled with any liquid, the

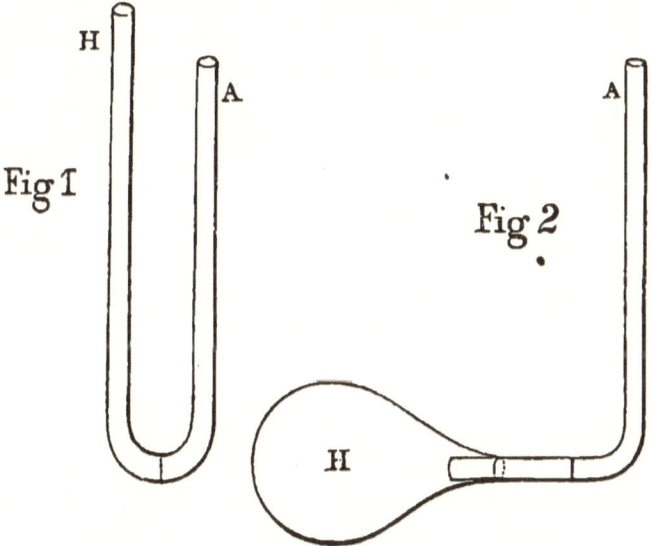

valve will be kept fast by the weight of a column of liquid 90 inches in height. Next pour liquid into the branch H, and the closure of the valve will become less and less firm as you pour, till at length when the liquid stands at the same level in both arms of the tube, the pressure on both sides of the valve will be equal. The resistance of the valve is thus exactly overcome, and whatever additional quantity of liquid be poured into the branch H, it will at once force open the valve, and keep it open till an equal quantity of liquid overflows from the top of the branch A, and the equilibrium is again re-established.

It is scarcely necessary to point out that if in place of the branch of the tube H we substitute a compressible flask (H, Fig. 2), filled with liquid, then the force employed in compressing the flask must be capable of overcoming the same resistance as the column of liquid in the branch (H, Fig. 1). It certainly by no means follows that the actual force put forth by the hand in compressing the flask, shall be exactly equal to the effect it produces, or the resistance overcome; for that is a question dependent on the mechanism through which the force is communicated.

Exactly the same holds of the left ventricle of the heart itself, which, whenever it sends blood into the aorta, must first exert a contractile power capable of counterbalancing the weight of a column of blood 90 inches in height and ·4187 of a square inch in area, or nearly 23 oz. avr. This is the effect which must be produced, whatever be the absolute force which the heart, acting through its own mechanism, is obliged to put forth to attain the end in view.

To understand how the hæmastatic column is the measure of the resistances which oppose the egress of the blood from the heart, we have only to consider that there would be no resistance, nor any hæmastatic column, if the blood were ejected into free space, or into an empty or half-filled tube; but as soon as any obstacle presents itself to the progress of the blood, it will first fill the tube completely, and then every fresh quantity of liquid injected must, to make space for itself, forcibly push onward the liquid already in the tube; and as liquids press equally in all directions, it will press laterally and upward with the same force that it does along the axis of the tube, and so will elevate the hæmastatic column till it exactly balances the resistance opposed to the progress of the blood.

With respect to the auxiliary forces, it is manifest that the muscular force of the blood-vessels, which exists chiefly in the small arteries, must, by diminishing their area, act as an obstacle to the progress of the blood, and will add to the height of the hæmastatic column, so that no separate estimation of it requires to be made.   Neither does the other auxiliary force, the atmospheric pressure towards the chest and heart, require any separate account; for it signally diminishes the resistance to the progress of the blood, and so renders the 'hæmastatic column less high than it would otherwise be.

Having now examined all the questions which we pointed out as necessarily preliminary, we are prepared to calculate the effective force of the left ventricle of the heart.

We have found that whenever the ventricle contracts, it has to put forth a force capable of balancing a resistance of nearly 23 oz. ; but that force serves merely to make the valve yield before any additional pressure, and so permit the passage of more blood : but we have still to estimate the force necessary to give the blood which passes a velocity of 10 inches per second, which we found to be the velocity with which it flows at the beginning of the aorta.

If the blood moved with a velocity such as its own weight, that is, the force of gravity would communicate, it would pass over $16\frac{1}{12}$ feet in a second, and acquire at the end of it a velocity of $32\frac{1}{6}$ feet per second; and if in any vessel filled with liquid to the depth of $16\frac{1}{12}$ feet, an aperture be made at the bottom, the liquid will issue from it with a velocity of $32\frac{1}{6}$ feet per second.   But the blood only moves with a velocity of 50 feet per minute, or 10 inches per second.   Now, as the velocities of liquids issuing from apertures at different depths are as the square roots of the depths, a column of no more than ·129533 of an inch in height will give an efflux with a velocity of 10 inches per second.   Hence, if in the apparatus (Fig. 1) the long branch of the tube were filled to the height 90·1295 inches, the branch A, being full or containing 90 inches, if the liquid in the long branch were maintained constantly at the same level, the valve would be kept open, and a constant efflux of 10 inches per second would be maintained, or a current equal to that emitted from the heart.

But an apparatus of which the moving power is a column of

liquid 90·1295 inches in height, and kept constantly at the same level, represents badly the action of the heart, which is intermittent; for the ventricle, after the period of contraction is over, remains quiescent for double that period, and so continues its rhythmic movement with alternate periods of action and repose. What change must be made on the moving power of our apparatus to make it harmonise with the intermittent action of the left ventricle of the heart? The two elements of which the moving power consists must be treated in opposite ways. The column of 90 inches destined to balance the resistances to the flow of the blood does not act constantly, but only while the aortic valve is open, or during one third of the period from one pulse to another. Hence, instead of being estimated as a constantly acting force it must be reduced to one third; which is effected simply by calculating the force of the heart only for the period of the contraction of the ventricle, and not for an entire pulsation. But it is quite the reverse with the other portion of the moving power, the column of ·1295 inch destined to give motion to the blood; for the same rate of motion must be maintained during the whole pulsation, while the moving force acts during only one third of the time. Hence, this part of the power must be so increased as to give the current a triple velocity, and so make up for the intermission of the propulsive action. But to give a triple velocity the column of liquid must be made nine times higher, and so becomes 1·165797.

Hence, the force put forth at every contraction of the left ventricle of the heart is equal to the weight of a column of blood 91·165797 inches in height and ·4187 inch in area.

		Inches.
Column balancing resistances	. .	90
Column communicating motion .	.	1·165797
		91·165797

		Grains.
Weight of former	. . . .	9,989·0370
Weight of latter	. . . .	129·2869
23 oz. +55·8179 =		10,118·3239

Poiseuille estimates the hæmastatic column in man as equal in weight to 7 feet 1 inch = 85 inches water = 80·952 blood.

$$80\cdot952$$
$$1\cdot165797$$
$$\overline{\hspace{2cm}}$$

Total column, $82\cdot117797 = 20\frac{3}{4} + 19$, or 21 oz. nearly.

Keeping between the estimates of these two trustworthy observers, we shall assume 22 oz. as the weight and 87 inches as the height of the hæmastatic column — numbers deviating from perfect equivalence only by a minute fraction, but which it is very important to retain as whole numbers, for the convenience of speech and facilitating our conceptions of the mode of action of the heart. Our conclusion so expressed, is that the heart at each contraction exerts a force which would be in equilibrium if counterbalanced by a weight of 22 oz. + 129 grs.; and that the mode in which this force is expended is most easily understood by supposing that we have a tube 87 inches in height, and ·4187 of an inch in base, that this tube is exactly filled with blood, and that at each contraction of the heart two additional ounces of blood are forced into it at the lower end, lifting the whole column over a space of 8 inches, and causing an equal overflow at the top. This represents accurately the labour of the human heart, and supplies us with two numbers to express it : the one, 22 oz., being the weight of the column of blood, and the other, 8 inches, the space over which the column is lifted. The former of these numbers denotes the resistance that has to be overcome in forcing 2 oz. of blood into the aorta and pushing before it the whole mass of blood in the blood-vessels; the latter, again, denotes the velocity with which the blood issues from the heart. Multiplying those two numbers together we obtain the momentum which the heart communicates to the blood; 220 oz. moving with a velocity of 8 inches during the period of a pulsation, or of 10 inches per second, or 50 feet per minute. This is equivalent to 176 oz. (22×8) lifted one inch, or 14·66 oz. lifted one foot, during the period of a pulsation, or of 65·9 foot-pounds in a minute, or 42·3 foot-tons in twenty-four hours.

Our task is not yet finished. We have still to confront the absolute force of the left ventricle of the heart, as we have already defined it, and the famous theorem of Hales by which the amount of that force has been demonstrated to be about half a hundredweight. Is this really true? Has the great Author of Nature, all of whose works are wonderful, and which, whenever they are within the grasp of the comprehension of man, are found to accomplish the most complicated ends by the simplest means—has He, in the construction of the human heart, so far deviated from His usual plan that, if we may say it without irreverence, He has placed in the very centre of the admirable fabric of the human body an organ so clumsily fashioned that it has to put forth the force of half a hundredweight to produce an effect which admits of being measured by a weight of $22\frac{1}{4}$ oz. less by 5 grs.? Philosophy exclaims that the supposition is derogatory to the wisdom of the Supreme Being, and therefore impious; and that the demonstration of Hales must be wrong. But in physical science it is not admissible to refute a mathematical demonstration by an *à priori* argument. We must meet Hales' reasoning fairly, on his own field and with his own weapons.

The effective force of a muscle in accomplishing a given end may be the same as its absolute force. This is obviously the case when a muscle of which all the fibres are parallel acts in a vertical direction upon a weight to be raised. But if the muscle act in an oblique direction, then its force is resolved into two parts, one acting vertically, and the other horizontally; of these only the former is effective in raising the weight, and so the effective force is less than the absolute by the amount of the horizontal force. Almost every machine of human construction is imperfect in this way, as the forces can seldom be so skilfully disposed as to tell directly on the centre of gravity of the parts to be moved. Does the same rule apply to the mechanism of the human heart—a hollow muscular organ expelling its contents by the contraction of its own parietes? Hales answers in the affirmative, and demonstrates it by applying to the heart the well-known principle of the hydrostatic paradox. The internal surface of the left ventricle of the heart is, according to his measurement, equal to 15 square inches. Now, when the heart contracts every part of this surface, equal to ·4187 of an inch is pressed upon by a weight of 22 oz., and must react with a force capable of overcoming that resistance. In 15 square inches there are 35·82 such spaces. Multiplying, therefore, 35·82 by 22 oz., we obtain a total force of almost exactly 49 lb. Hales' own calculation gives 51 lb., and Dr Arnott's 60 lb.

I join with the speculative philosophers in the full conviction that there must be some error underlying the ingenious application which Hales has made of his own experiments to demonstrate the above proposition. But it is more easy to suspect than to point out and rectify that error.

In the experimental demonstration of the hydrostatic paradox it would be a fatal error if, in the vessel into which is inserted the tube regulating the hydrostatic pressure and which ought to be a vessel everywhere shut, there existed an opening of ·4187 of an inch in size; for in that case the liquid would flow out through the opening, and the lateral pressure, being diminished, the column of liquid in the tube would subside. Now, this is exactly what happens in the heart. If, as we have supposed, the length of the systole of the heart be one third of a second, and no blood were to escape from the ventricle during that period, the calculation of Hales would be exact. But if the blood escape, as it actually does, through an aperture of ·4187 of an inch, then the lateral pressure upon the walls of the ventricle must become gradually less as the blood flows away, and the hæmastatic column must subside in proportion. Now, according to the testimony of Hales himself, and of all subsequent observers, the hæmastatic column rises to its full height at the commencement of the contraction of the ventricles, and then immediately begins to subside. Observation thus proves the truth of what reasoning suggests, that the blood escaping along the aorta must gradually diminish the tension on the walls of the ventricle. There is at first an enormous strain upon the heart till it communicates the impulse to the blood and sets it in motion, and much less force is thereafter required to keep it going : just as we see a loaded waggon require at first an enormous force to set it in motion, while it goes on smoothly thereafter with a very small force superadded to its acquired momentum.

It is thus manifest that the lateral pressure against the walls of the ventricle gradually diminishes from the beginning to the end of the systole, and that the force necessary to overcome that resistance must in like manner diminish, being converted into the momentum of the moving current of blood. Now, the principal cause of the excess, in the estimate of Hales, is that he supposes the initial force of the ventricle to continue undiminished during the whole period of the systole. But there is another cause not less apparent, which is, that he supposes the area of the surface of the ventricle to continue throughout at 15 square inches, whereas it gradually diminishes, till finally it disappears altogether as the last particle of blood is expelled.

The knowledge which we now possess of the laws of muscular contractility, as deduced from the experiments of Schwann, enable us to estimate with some degree of certainty the amount of both those causes of error and so to rectify the whole calculation.

When a fully extended muscular fibre begins to contract it exerts its utmost force, and as the contraction goes on the force gradually diminishes, being always denoted by the remaining fraction of the difference in length between the fully contracted and the fully distended fibre. The mean force of a muscle is thus one half of the initial force in muscles of which the fibres run all in one direction; one fourth of it in muscles of which the fibres are uniformly disposed in different directions in the same membranous plane; and one eighth of it in solid muscular organs having fibres running equably in all directions.

We conclude, therefore, that the mean force of the muscular fibres, as arranged in the human heart, is no more than one eighth of their original force; and we know the amount of that original force as determined by Hales: for it cannot be doubted that if the surface of the ventricle of the heart measures 15 square inches, and the weight of the hæmastatic column be correctly estimated at 22 oz., then, at the very instant of time when the ventricle begins to contract and for an infinitesimal period, it must exert a force of not less than 49 lb. But that force does not continue at the same rate throughout, but gradually diminishes till it vanishes altogether, and when at its mean rate is no more than one eighth of what it originally was.

Having thus reduced to its proper magnitude one of the factors in Hales' calculation, we must endeavour to do the same with his other factor—the size of the ventricular surface, which we shall suppose to be correctly estimated by him at 15 square inches in the distended heart. But he falls into an error quite analogous to the one we have just been considering when he supposes the ventricular surface to continue undiminished during the whole systole, while in reality it becomes less and less as the blood is expelled from the ventricle till it vanishes altogether, when the cavity is completely empty and obliterated.

Our object, then, is to determine what is the size of the ventricular surface at the point of time when the contractile power of the heart has diminished to one eighth. Now, this can be done without difficulty if we are permitted to assume, what seems probable, that the diminution of the surface of the ventricle as the blood is expelled from it and the ratio which it bears to the blood which still remains to be expelled may be estimated in the same way in which we estimate the area and cubic contents of a spherical cavity gradually diminishing in size till it finally vanishes.

To show this draw the lines D and d, making d equal to one half of D; next describe two circles, having their diameters equal to D and d respectively; and lastly, draw two spheres, of which the diameters are equal to the same lines D and d respectively.

The line D, on which the size of all the other lines both straight and circular depends, represents the difference in length between a muscular fibre fully extended and the same fibre fully contracted. It follows from what has been said above that as the muscular fibre contracts the line D

2

FIG. 2, *bis.*

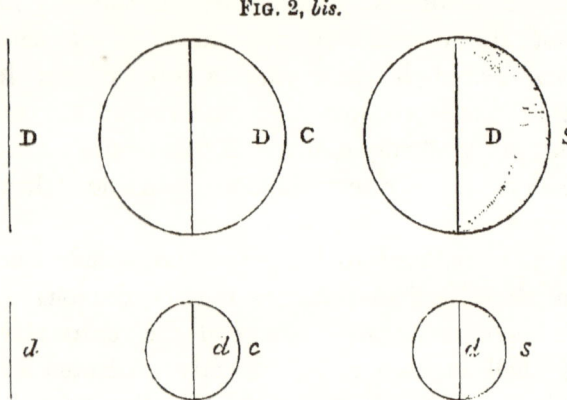

diminishes, and the part of it remaining always denotes the amount of force remaining in the fibre. But in a muscle of which all the fibres are parallel, if the initial force be represented by the line D, the mean force will be represented by the line *d*, for by construction *d* is equal to one half of D ; in like manner, in a muscle of which the fibres are equably disposed in different directions in the same membranous plane, if the circle D C represent the initial force, the circle *d c* will represent the mean force, for *d c* is one fourth of D C ; and lastly, in a solid muscular organ, like the heart, having fibres acting in all directions, if the sphere D S represent the initial force, the sphere *d s* will represent the mean force, for the sphere *d s* is equal to one eighth of D S.

Still farther, the superficial area of the sphere *d s* is just the fourth part of the area of the sphere D S.   The area of the ventricle of the heart, therefore, instead of being estimated as continuing throughout at 15 square inches, must be estimated at the fourth part of that amount.

It thus appears that the initiatory power of the heart diminishes rapidly from two separate and independent causes ; that by the one it diminishes on attaining a medium to one fourth, and by the other to one eighth.   Combining these two ratios, we have a total medium estimate of one thirty-second $(\frac{1}{32})$.*

* If the line D denote the difference in length of a spiral fibre of the heart when extended and when fully contracted ; and if the line *d* varying as the fibre

Now, if we multiply 22 oz. by 32, the result is 44 lb., which would be very nearly the initiatory power of the heart, if we assume the size of the ventricular surface as 13·3984 square inches, intermediate between the measurement of Hales at fifteen, and that of Arnott at ten square inches. The conclusion therefore is, that there is no difference between the effective force of the heart estimated at 22 oz., and the mean absolute force = $\frac{44}{32}$ lb. or 704 oz. divided by 32 = 22 oz. This is in exact accordance with the general economy of nature, as we see it displayed in the muscular system. In the articular movements she sacrifices muscular energy profusely whenever there is an adequate object to be attained, such as extent and facility of movement, or even the symmetry of the parts to be moved. But whenever a great weight is to be lifted, as in locomotion, and other great bodily exertions, she is wisely economical of her muscular force. The same law holds good in the most important of all the actions of the involuntary muscles—the never-ceasing action of the heart—in which the precise amount of muscular power is expended which is necessary for the end in view.

contracts always denotes the difference between the actual length of the fibre and its length when fully contracted; then will the expulsive force of the heart at any point of time between the commencement and the termination of the systole be denoted by d^5, for it is equal to $d^3 \times d^2 = d^5$. Whence, if the mean force of the fibre be to the initial force as 1 : 2, the mean expulsive force will be to the initial force as 1 : 2^5 = 1 : 32.

PART II

THE VASCULAR FORCES

As the remaining part of our subject was only taken up with reference to the force of the heart, it might have been passed over with the slight notice already given, were it not that it is a subject of great interest in itself,—and still more, that we cannot fully apprehend the part which the heart plays in the circulation of the blood without knowing whether and to what extent it derives assistance from other forces.

The mass of blood to be moved is about an eighth part of the weight of the human body, or 17¼ lb. in a man of 10 stones in weight; and the following table gives a synoptical view of the velocity of the current of blood in the various parts of the sanguiferous circuit :—

VELOCITY OF BLOOD.

	Per minute.	
	Inches.	Feet. Inches.
Root of aorta	600	= 50 —
Mean arterial current	39	= 3 3·84
Onward motion in network of capillaries	2·64	= — 2·64
Mean venous current	24·36 =	2 0·36
End of venæ cavæ	205	= 17 1

There are three forces mainly concerned in carrying on the circulation of the blood.   These are :—1st. A central pro- pulsive force.   2nd. The muscular contractility of the blood- vessels ; and 3rd. A central pneumatic force , or the atmo- spheric pressure toward the chest and heart, rendered effective by a central dilative force. Of these the second is in the human system comparatively insignificant, while the first and last divide between them the labour of carrying on the circulation of the blood in proportions not differing much, as we shall hereafter endeavour to show, from 3 to 2.

The central propulsive power consists in a triple series of muscular contractions,—those of the great venous trunks, of the auricles, and of the ventricles, which take place rhythmically in the order of succession just indicated. The first two of those forces are expended in maintaining the circulation through the heart itself. We have therefore only to consider the propulsive force of the ventricles, and chiefly that of the left ventricle, which is more powerful than the right, as might be expected from its structure, and from the greater distance and more numerous and denser tissues to which it has to propel the blood. Our most certain information, with respect to the relative force of the right ventricle, is derived from an observation of Hering, which he had the opportunity of making on the heart of a calf affected with congenital ectopia of that organ. He found the height of the hæmastatic column in the right ventricle to be to that of the column in the left as 1 to 1·7; so that the propulsive power of the left ventricle must be to that of the right as 10 to 7·64 nearly. We know also that the area of the pulmonary artery is greater than that of the aorta, so that the blood must move more slowly through it in the same proportion. To the force of the left ventricle, the mode in which it is expended, and the velocity with which the blood issues from it, we need not return.

We cannot, however, but advert to this same force as it appears under an altered form after the blood has been injected into the arteries, and comes under the influence of the elastic coat of these vessels. The elasticity of the arteries never can be regarded as a primary moving power of the blood, as it imparts no new force, but merely reflects the force imparted by the heart. In this way it serves two most important purposes. In the first place, it equalises and renders continuous the intermittent force of the heart, substituting for it an uniformly acting force, which controls the irregular movement of the blood, and propels it in an uniform stream through the smaller arteries, the capillaries, and the veins,—moderating, at the same time, the shock which it communicates to the tissues, as it permeates them. Hales* has very aptly compared the elasticity of the arteries to the elasticity of the air in a forcing pump, which, acting with an uniform pressure on the surface of the liquid, impels it in a steady and equable stream, however irregular the force may have been by which it was introduced into the reservoir. At page 38 will be seen the description of an apparatus in which gravity is substituted for the elasticity of the arteries, and plays exactly the same part, returning in an equable form the whole force delegated to it by the intermittent contractions of the pump.

The other purpose served by the elasticity of the arteries is not less important,—indeed, without it the circulation of the blood in the remote peripheral circuits could not be carried on. It propagates the force derived from the heart unabated throughout the whole arterial system, so that arteries of equal size, whether near to or remote from the heart, propel the blood with the same force into the capillary vessels in which they terminate. Poisseuille has shown that in all arteries the hæmastatic column stands at the same height, there being an equilibrium of tension throughout the whole arterial system. The whole arterial blood may therefore be regarded as contained in a single reservoir, surrounded everywhere by the same elastic membrane, and everywhere pressed upon with equal force. In this way the force of the heart, instead of ceasing at the extremities of the arterial system, as some physiologists have supposed, is, as it were, delegated to the terminal arteries, enabling them to press the blood with equal force into their corresponding veins. This provision is rendered necessary by the great inequality in the length of the circuits by which the blood supplied to different parts returns to the heart. Without it the blood would return in a full stream through the most direct channels, and would stagnate in those more remote,—just as we see in a river where it spreads wide, the main current is in the middle, while at the

* 'Hæmastaticks,' vol. ii, p. 23.

sides it revolves in eddies or completely stands still. It will, however, be seen hereafter that the pneumatic forces exercise an important influence over the circulation through the capillaries.

The second moving power, above mentioned, is the muscular contractility of the blood-vessels. Whether the arteries, in addition to the physical contractility which enables them to reflect and modify the force of the heart, possess also a vital contractility capable of communicating an original and independent impulse to the blood, was much discussed among the physiologists of the last age. The numerous arguments adduced on the affirmative side had already, in general estimation, decided this question, when the discovery of muscular fibres in the coats of the blood-vessels, and more especially in the smaller arteries, finally removed all doubt with respect to it. Still further, recent investigations have shown the muscular fibres of the blood-vessels to be, like other muscles, under the control of the nervous system. Muscular fibres are found in the coats both of the arteries and of the veins, but most abundant in the former. They are likewise much more abundant in the small arteries than in those of larger size. The capillary vessels alone are devoid of them. Hence, these last vessels are regarded as mere passive channels of transmission, except in so far as they are modified by the relaxation or contraction of the tissues in which they are distributed, while all the rest are believed to possess more or less of a vital contractility, capable of imparting a fresh impulse to the blood as it passes through them. The action of the muscular fibres of the blood-vessels, like that of other unstriped muscles, is of the tonic kind, persisting for a certain period after being once excited. The effect of it is in the first instance to empty out the blood-vessels of a certain quantity of the blood which they contain, and thereafter to make them receive a less quantity of blood so long as the contraction continues. The muscular fibres of the arteries act by increasing or diminishing the tension of the elastic coat, but the effect on the movement of the blood is the same, for it is so distributed in the neighbouring arteries as to maintain everywhere among them an equilibrium of tension. Just in the same way, if two separate air-chambers acted on the same mass of liquid, a force acting by expanding or condensing the air in one air-chamber would immediately occasion a fresh distribution of the liquid, till equilibrium was restored.

But a further question remains for discussion. To what use does nature intend the muscular power of the blood-vessels to be applied? Is it as a constantly acting force to assist in the progressive movement of the blood; or does it merely serve a secondary purpose, meeting the contingencies that present themselves in particular parts, and so regulating the local distribution of the blood? We may, I think, safely reply to this question, that while nature often does apply the muscular power of vascular tubes to answer the former purpose, yet in the sanguiferous vessels of man and the higher animals it is applied solely, or almost solely, for the latter purpose.

In the lower animals, destitute of a heart (if we except the very lowest), the muscular power of the blood-vessels supplies its place, and in the lymphatic vessels of man the lymph is propelled into the venous system by the same power. But whenever this occurs, we at once recognise it by two conditions, the presence of one or other, or of both of which is indispensable to the effectual working of the contracting tubes. Either the tubes must be everywhere plentifully furnished with valves, or there must be a regular rhythm in their contractile action, corresponding to the direction in which the fluid is to be propelled. It must be obvious that without those conditions the contraction of any vessel would force the liquid within it as much backward as forward, and most readily in whatever direction the resistance was least.

The presence of valves in any part of the circulating system certainly indicates the action at that part of a force capable of producing retrogressive movement. But vascular contraction is not the only such force, for the same effect results from compression of the vessels, whether by external force or by the action of circumjacent muscles. But these cases are easily distinguished by the much less extensive distribution of the valves in the latter cases than in the former. Whenever a liquid is impelled through a set of tubes by vascular contraction aided by valves, those valves will be found thickly set in the whole or great majority of those tubes. Such is the structure of the lymphatic vessels, and, in consequence, we infer that the lymph is propelled mainly in these vessels by the contraction of their muscular fibres; which, among reptiles, are assisted by the organs named lymphatic hearts. In the blood-vessels, on the contrary, we find valves almost only in the superficial veins which are exposed to external pressure or the compression of contracting muscles, while the absence of valves in the deep-seated veins, in the capillaries, and in the arteries, disproves in so far the action of the muscular fibres of the vessels as a cause of the progressive movement of the blood; and the disproval becomes complete when we find that there is no rhythmic movement of the fluids in the veins, capillaries, and smaller arteries. The only rhythmic movement observed in the vascular system is that originating in the heart. It is counteracted by the elasticity of the arteries, and does not usually extend to the end of the arterial system, unless the vessels be distended with blood, when it stretches into the capillaries, as may be at any time seen under the microscope in the web of the frog's foot, by obstructing the flow of blood through the veins of the limb.

The conclusion here drawn, that the use of the muscular fibres of the blood-vessels is to regulate the local distribution of the blood, is quite in accordance with the recent experiments on the nervous system, which have been interpreted as producing palsy of the vaso-motor nerves of particular parts; for the effect is not to obstruct the circulation in these parts, but to cause a permanent afflux of blood towards them, which they are no longer able to get rid of.

The doctrine of Bichât, that the force of the heart extends no farther than the end of the arteries, and that the blood receives a new impulse from the capillary vessels to carry it onward to the heart, is disproved by the structure of those vessels, which shows them to be incompetent for such an action. It is disproved also by the experiments of Magendie, showing that the interruption or retardation of the blood in the crural artery is indicated instantaneously by a corresponding interruption or retardation of the blood in the crural vein, and proving manifestly that there is no intermediate force which has the slightest influence over the stream.

Many physiologists, following the late Dr Allison of Edinburgh, adopt the theory that the blood is urged onward through the extreme vessels, in which the arterial and venous systems communicate, by a force originating in the physical and chemical actions going on in the tissues of the lungs on the one hand, and of the general system on the other. Some of them suppose "the oxygen in the pulmonary cells" to have an attraction for blood in the venous state, but none for blood in the arterial state, whence the venous blood is drawn along the pulmonary capillaries, and drives the arterial blood before it; but this attraction being reversed in the systemic capillaries, it is the arterial blood which is drawn along them, and now in its turn drives the venous blood before it. To this doctrine the great objection is that it is a pure figment of the imagination, as there are no forces, physical or physiological, known to exist in nature, which could possibly produce the effects here referred to. But some physiologists do not go so far, and they are entitled to a candid hearing so long as they keep within the recognised limits of mechanical science, and propose merely to transfer to the animal economy principles which are held to afford an explanation of the circulation of plants.

There is a great contrast between the circulation of plants and that of animals. In the latter the blood moves with great rapidity within distinct vessels, and always in the same direction from the heart to the heart again. In the former the sap moves very slowly, in vessels or other channels by no means well defined; sometimes in one direction, sometimes in the opposite, but never in a course to which the name of circulation can be strictly applied, for it is a mere progression from one part of the plant to another. The rapidity of the current in animals is indispensable for the supply of the nervous and muscular tissues; while in plants, where these tissues do not exist, the movement of the sap serves merely for the elaboration of the nutrient fluid, and the conversion of it into tissues and other products of nutrition.

Passing over the less perfect vegetable forms, it is enough for our purpose to speak of the movement of the sap in the trees of our own country, in which it has been most success- fully investigated. In these it exhibits, annually, three remarkable phases,—differing from each other in the season of their occurrence, in the physiological objects which they serve, and in the mechanism by which they are effected.

The first occurs in the spring, and serves for the develop- ment of the buds, the elongation of the stem and branches, and the evolution of the leaves. It is effected almost entirely by the force of osmosis. All that capillarity has to do with it is to take the first step by introducing water into the tissues of the root, expanded by the first heat of the season. But no sooner is the liquid introduced than it acts through the inter- vening membrane on the inspissated juice, deposited for that very purpose at the end of the preceding year in the cells of the plant; an active osmosis ensues, the liquid rising in the sap vessels and other pervious channels exactly as it does in the tube of an osmometer. Such is the force with which it is pressed upward that in the vine it has been found, in the spring, to counterbalance a column of mercury 38 inches in height, equal to 43 feet 3½ inches of water*—a performance quite equal to that of a good osmometer. If, again, a branch of any size be wounded, as by cutting it across, a copious dis- charge of sap ensues, sometimes so great as even to endanger the life of the plant, and hence the period, when this move- ment is going on, has been named the bleeding season. This movement does not cease entirely on the exhaustion of the inspissated sap contained in the stem, for it may continue during the whole season, the leaves first developed supplying the inspissated juice by which the further growth is kept up. This is what happens in annual plants, in which, when they begin to grow, the supply reposited in the cotyledons of the seed acts the same part as the annual deposit in the stems of

* Hales, vol. i, p. 124.

trees, and thereafter the leaves, as they are successively developed, act the same part as fresh cotyledons.

The second phase of the sap-movement is subservient to the functions of the leaf, and is at its height when the leaves are fully expanded during the summer months. The crude sap absorbed by the root is carried to the leaves to be converted into the true sap (succus proprius) of the plant. The liquid rises through the sap-vessels as far as the leaves by capillary attraction, assisted probably to a small extent by the force of osmosis; but that the latter force is comparatively insignificant, is manifest from the fact that bleeding now no longer takes place on the plant being wounded, for any fluid within the sap-vessels is retained there by capillary attraction instead of being protruded, as would have happened from osmosis. But these forces could produce no continuous ascending movement of the sap were the sap-vessels not continually emptied out at their upper ends by the exhalation from the surface of the leaves, occasioned by the temperature and dryness of the ambient air. The apparatus described by Liebig, consisting of a glass tube filled with water, having its upper orifice covered by a bit of bladder, while the lower is immersed in a vessel of water, illustrates the moving force in this form of the circulation of plants, as an ascending current is maintained in the glass tube by the continual evaporation from the surface of the bladder. We have another familiar illustration in Bergson's spray-maker, in which the liquid to be converted into spray and vapour is continually carried off from the orifice of an upright capillary tube, and so causes a rapid ascent of the liquid in the tube by which it is supplied.

The third phase in the movement of the sap is the converse of the first. It occurs in the autumn, when the leaves have completed the elaboration of the proper sap. They now no longer exhale moisture but absorb it,—a change in their action which is in harmony with the increased moisture and diminished temperature of the external air. But the water is no sooner absorbed than it reacts physically upon the inspissated juice reposited in the leaves, and an active osmosis ensues. The current sets chiefly downward, assisted by gravity, and goes to form the new layers of wood and bark, in which the superfluous portion of it is reposited in preparation for the osmosis upward in the ensuing spring. A portion of the sap, however, goes upward to form the seeds, and the whole of it may do so, as in annual plants. An interesting result as well as an evidence of the descending current being caused by osmosis, is that the phenomenon of bleeding from wounds again presents itself, but with this difference, that the flow is from above and not from below, as in the spring. This is well seen in the process for collecting the resinous juice of the pine by cutting the trunk of the tree near the ground about half-way across and obliquely downward, while a chamber is excavated in the part of the trunk beneath to receive the descending juice.

But to return to our argument. Of the three phases of the circulation in plants described above, the first and the last, which are the results of osmosis, are not attended by any sensible movement of the sap unless there be some accidental outlet for it, as by a wound, which bleeds upward in the spring and downward in the autumn. But in normal circumstances, when once the vessels have been filled, there is merely an insensible movement of the sap, which is urged by a powerful expansive force into the soft substance of the growing tissues. Such a movement cannot be compared with the continuous movement of the blood in animals. The second or summer phase again presents a continuous flow of the sap from the roots to the leaves, and can be readily compared with the circulation in animals. Now, the quantity of sap which flows upward depends entirely upon the quantity of vapour which is exhaled from the leaves, and by measuring this exhalation vegetable physiologists have been enabled to determine the quantity of sap which flows along the stem in a given time. Thus, in a sunflower $3\frac{1}{2}$ feet in height, and having a transverse area of a square inch in the middle of the stem, Hales found 20 ounces of sap to pass upward through the stem in twelve hours during the day.* Now, the lungs are to animals what

* 'Vegetable Staticks,' p. 7.

the leaves are to plants. We know also the amount of exhalation (comprehending under that name both the watery vapour
and carbonic acid gas) which takes place from the pulmonary
mucous membrane in man to be about 40 oz., or 2½ lb., in the
twenty-four hours, or just about double that which takes place
in the sunflower, for plants during the night exhale very little
moisture, and often absorb it. But what can be inferred from
this comparison? Simply that two and a half pounds of liquid
pass along the pulmonary artery in 24 hours. Now, the quantity of blood which actually passes along the pulmonary artery
is 17½ lb. in two minutes. Even, therefore, if the exhalation
from the lungs were as influential over the circulation of the
blood as the exhalation from the leaves unquestionably is over
the movement of the sap, the small quantity of the pulmonary
exhalation, when compared with the vast torrent of the circulating blood, renders it utterly insignificant, considered as a
moving power.

PART III

THE PNEUMATIC FORCES

SECTION 1.— *General Principles*

THE third moving power of the sanguiferous system, and almost the only one worthy of being taken into account along with the propulsive force of the heart, is the pressure of the atmosphere towards the thorax and heart, in each of which there exists an active dilative force which the pressure of the atmosphere counteracts, and thus propels the blood onward to restore the equlibrium.

Incredulity of British physiologists as to pneumatic forces.— On no subject within the bounds of physiology or of medicine does such a diversity and inconsistency of opinion prevail among medical men as with respect to the above-mentioned force.   If you ask them if they believe in the existence of such a force, they will probably reply, with Dr Arnott, that it is " physically impossible," and perhaps add with a sneer, that such a belief could only enter into the minds of men ignorant of the first principles of mechanics.   If you ask them again if they believe in the danger of laying open veins, in performing operations in the vicinity of the heart, they will reply, without hesitation, that well-authenticated cases are on record in which atmospheric air has entered veins laid open by such operations, and passing on to the heart has caused death, just as happens from the forcible insufflation of air into the veins.   Still further, it will surprise some of the veterans of the profession who, in their younger days, when venesection was still held as a remedy in the healing art, were in the habit daily of performing that operation—it will surprise them, as it did me, to be informed

that the ribbon, which they in their simplicity conceived to
be bound round the arm merely to intercept the refluent blood,
is of use for the still higher purpose of preventing the atmospheric air from entering the vein, and so being transmitted to
the heart.*   Such an occurrence from the wound of a superficial
vein of the arm I believe to be impossible, from the multitude
of collateral channels through which the blood has free access
to the heart.   But even if the reasoning be erroneous, it still
shows, on the part of our surgeons, a firm belief in a physiological doctrine which is formally repudiated or timidly ignored
by the leading physiologists of this country.

Causes of this incredulity.   The hostility of Dr Arnott.—This
unsettled state of medical opinion, as it exists only among our-
selves, must have originated in local causes.   It appears to me
to be satisfactorily explained by the influence on the one hand
of the ingenious arguments and experiments of Dr Carson and
Sir David Barry, and on the other of the sweeping denunciation
of their opinions contained in Dr Arnott's work on Natural
Philosophy,† a work which has exercised a powerful influence
on the minds of medical men on most subjects where physiology
rests on the basis of physics.   On the present occasion that
influence has been very great and permanent.   Whether it was
merely that Dr Arnott regarded the new doctrine as an unwarranted innovation on the venerable teachings of Harvey,
whose disciple he professes himself to be, or whether he had
other causes of antipathy against it or its abettors, I cannot say,
but certainly he has spared no pains in his endeavours to
exterminate it.   He does not merely seek to persuade his
readers by the force of his arguments, but to carry them away
by the authority of his name, or terrify them into submission
by the violence of his criticism.   Even Dr Arnott's warmest
admirers (of whom I have always been one) cannot but regret
the spirit in which he has carried on this controversy, the
supercilious dogmatism with which he enunciates his own
opinions, and the immeasurable contempt, or rather pity,

* I have known several abettors of this opinion, although I am not aware
whether it has been made public through the press.

† Second Edition, 1825.

which he ostentatiously bestows on his two antagonists, and on the whole medical profession, as participating in their ignorance and credulity.*

His general objection to all forms of pneumatic agency.—Dr Arnott's great name, and the general acquiescence in his opinions, which it has procured for him from the medical public in this country, render it necessary for me to consider his objections fully. Some of them will be best discussed along with those parts of our argument to which they respectively correspond; but there is one which seems to me entitled to a preliminary discussion, as it is an objection of a general kind, not applying to one part only, but to the whole of our subject; and, if valid, rendering all further discussion unnecessary, as it is subversive of the doctrine of pneumatic agency, under whatever form it can assume.

Fallacy of Dr Arnott's reasoning.—The objection is that the veins are pliant tubes, which collapse on the slightest pressure applied to them. This, according to Dr Arnott, " proves it to be a physical impossibility that a sucking action of the heart or chest can be a cause of the blood's motion along the veins." No pump, he says truly, can lift liquid through such pliant tubes. If any one were to attach a syringe to a piece of gut or eel skin, or vein, and be so foolish as to try to draw up water through them, the attempt would be frustrated by the immediate collapse of the tubes. Dr Arnott's premises are undeniable, but his conclusion is not the less illogical. He argues from one set of physical conditions to another, which is totally dissimilar. In the case supposed above, there is only one force in action, the pressure of the atmosphere, which causes the tube to collapse; as there is no other force to oppose it and keep the tube distended. In the veins of a living man, again, there are two forces in action, which Dr Arnott has overlooked: the force of the heart and the pressure of the atmosphere. These two forces are so wisely adapted to each other that, while

* In the last edition of his work, Dr Arnott, while he adheres to his conclusions, omits the whole argument from which they are derived. His readers would have been better pleased if he had repeated the argument, merely omitting the offensive passages which disfigure it in the former edition.

both of them propel the blood along the veins, each of them prevents the inconveniences and danger that would have resulted singly from the action of the other. If the atmospheric pressure were to act alone, the circulation would be at once arrested by the collapse of the veins. If, again, the force of the heart were the sole moving power, the veins would be continually in a state of dangerous over-distension and obstruction. The combination of the two forces completely obviates these dangers and inconveniences, for the veins in the state of health are kept always moderately full without the risk of over-distension on the one hand, or of collapse on the other.

It is admitted, on all sides, that the blood-vessels are in an eminent degree susceptible of the influence of atmospheric pressure, as they are, for the most part, exposed to it at every point, either directly, like the superficial veins, or indirectly through the soft parts in which they are embedded. The vessels which pass through bony channels, or lie within the cranium, are less exposed; but are still acted upon through their free extremities, like the rigid tubes in any ordinary hydraulic apparatus. These remarks, it is to be observed, apply not to the veins only, but to the whole blood-vessels of the body, arteries, capillaries, and veins. It is a great error, leading, as will be seen below, to the misinterpretation of many important physiological phenomena, to conceive the effects of the pressure of the atmosphere to be confined to the veins in the vicinity of the chest.

It is farther admitted, on both sides of this discussion, that if a pump be attached to a flaccescent tube full of liquid, and that liquid be not simultaneously influenced by any propulsive force, the effect of the action of the pump will be only transitory; for, as soon as the tube is emptied of liquid it will collapse, and render all further action of the pump a physical impossibility. But, if any propulsive force be in simultaneous operation, then, it is here contended—1st, that the continuous action of the pump is quite possible, so long as it is not too powerful, that is, so long as it is kept within the limits of the physical conditions indicated generally above, and particularly defined farther down ; and, 2nd, that the continuous action of the pump so employed is signally effective in promoting the flow of liquid through the tube, whatever may be its length, however great may be its thickness, and whatever, within certain limits, may be its tenuity, or to whatever extent it may be divided into branches, and these again united into a single tube, the whole constituting two arborescent systems of tubes, like the blood-vessels of an animal body. The time taken up with this discussion is not, therefore lost, since it enables us to determine the general laws according to which pneumatic forces operate within the living body ; or, in other words, under what physical conditions, and with what mutual limitations, a propulsive and a pneumatic force can be of use in promoting the flow of liquid through membranous tubes.

Physical conditions under which pneumatic forces act on flaccescent tubes.

(1) *As auxiliaries to a propulsive force.*—The first general law is that already stated, that every pneumatic force must necessarily be accompanied by a constantly acting propulsive force. Hence it is clear, that a pneumatic force never can be more than an auxiliary force, and never can be the prime and sole moving power ; for there must necessarily be a propulsive force acting from behind ; or, what is usually termed a *vis à tergo*, to keep the flaccescent tubes from collapsing, as they must necessarily do if the propulsive force were to cease altogether or become too feeble to keep the tubes distended.

(2) *Limit of momentum communicated to liquid is that given by propulsive force.*—A second general law is, that pneumatic forces, or, in other words, the pressure of the atmosphere, never can give to the blood a momentum greater than the propulsive force alone is capable of communicating. The propulsive force keeps the coats of the vessels distended ; the pressure of the atmosphere forces them inwards in the opposite direction ; and if the latter force predominate over the former, immediate shrinking, and at length collapse, must ensue. We have only, therefore, to determine the amount of the propulsive force, to determine also the limit within which the atmospheric pressure can promote the circulation without the risk of interrupting it. Now, the propulsive force in any blood-vessel is accurately

measured by the height of the hæmastatic column which it supports. By turning to the Table at p. 8, it will be seen that in all the great arteries of the body the hæmastatic column stands at the height of 90 inches. The weight of such a column must press upon every square inch of the internal surface of the arteries, and keep it distended with a force of $3\frac{1}{4}$ lb. (3 lb. $6\frac{1}{4}$ oz.). In the jugular vein, near the cardiac end of the circuit, the height of the column is nine inches, so that the vein is still kept distended with a pressure of upwards of a quarter of a pound (5·453 oz.) on every square inch of its inner surface. If, therefore, a pump be attached to any large artery, or to the jugular vein, the above numbers indicate, respectively, the utmost momentum which the action of the pump can communicate to the blood without risk of interrupting the circulation. But a much greater force, and even the whole pressure of the atmosphere may be required to communicate to the blood the momentum just indicated, as will be seen from what follows.

(3) *If no excess of momentum, any amount of pneumatic force available.*—The third general law, or rather principle, is, that as long as the current resulting from the propulsive force suffers no interruption, either by the failure of the force from behind or by the two rapid subduction of liquid from before, so long will the pressure of the atmosphere, whatever be its amount, cause only a forward and never a retrogressive movement of the liquid, and so it will become signally effective in removing obstructions to the progress of the liquid.

It is manifest that if there were no propulsive force the liquid would be forced by the pressure of the atmosphere alike forward and backward; but if there be a propulsive force, then the forces acting in a forward direction exceed the force acting backwards exactly by the amount of the propulsive force, and this holds whatever be the amount of the atmospheric pressure; and hence, any amount of that pressure becomes available for overcoming resistances.

Among the obstructions which the atmospheric pressure is capable of removing, may be comprehended those to which the name of normal may be applied, as proceeding from the physical properties of the blood, as from its mass and weight;

or from the natural structure of the blood-vessels, their length, their largeness, their tortuous course, their division and sub-division, their ramification in capillary networks, and their sub-sequent reunion into large venous trunks. Over all of these the pressure of the atmosphere exercises a signal influence so long as it is kept within the limits indicated above. There are even certain accidental obstructions, as the complete occlusion of one or more vessels by compression, or from pathological causes, which can be overcome by the atmospheric pressure, provided there be free passage for the blood through collateral channels.

Apparatus illustrative of the operation of pneumatic force on flaccescent tubes, and of their utility.—This subject will be best illustrated by reference to an apparatus so constructed as to imitate the two great physical conditions under which the cir-culation of the blood is carried on : viz. (1st.) the influence of the action of the heart, at first direct and therefore inter-mittent, but afterwards delegated and so rendered uniform by the elasticity of the arteries; and (2nd) the influence of the pressure of the atmosphere urging the blood in the same direction.

To imitate the uniform propulsive force with which the blood is urged along the jugular vein, I placed a funnel, supported on a stand, with its upper orifice from 9 to 10 inches from the floor of a leaden cistern ; and I so adjusted, by means of a stop-cock, the supply of water from a pipe above, that the funnel was kept constantly full without overflowing. I next attached to the lower end of the funnel a portion of lamb's gut twelve feet in length. I took it so long that it might be longer than the whole vascular system, but a much shorter portion is less inconvenient, and answers all the purposes of illustration. In whatever way the gut was placed, if there was no twist in it, the water flowed out at its farthest end without interruption. I now attached a pump to this farther end, and found that it worked with the most perfect facility,—just as great as if the pump had been placed in an open vessel of water. This was the case whether I used a cylinder and piston, the former holding from 1 to 2 oz., or, what I preferred, as being more like the heart an elastic caoutchouc bag holding more than 2 oz.

Stopping the supply from above, I now used the apparatus so as to give an exact representation, according to my views, of the two great forces which keep up the circulation of the blood, and also of the force which acts so beautifully in converting the

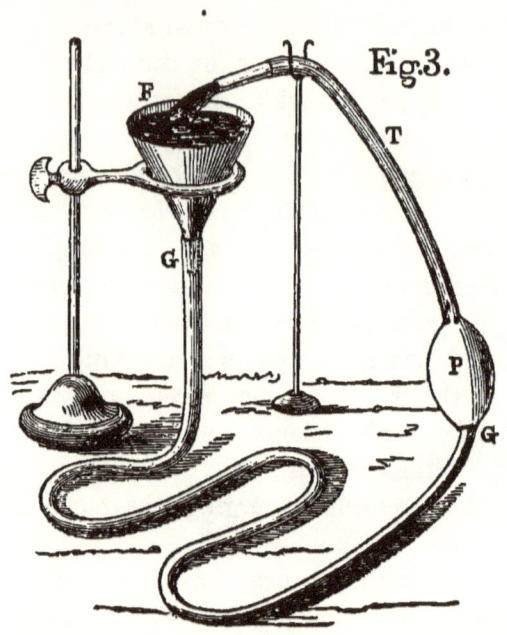

Fig. 3.

intermittent stream into a uniform one. This arrangement is represented in Fig. 3, where F represents the funnel full of liquid, G G, the lamb's gut lying on the floor of the cistern, P, the caoutchouc pump, and T, a flexible tube rising above the level of the funnel, so as to return the liquid into it. This apparatus works with perfect facility, and exhibits a most instructive view of the three forces mainly concerned in the circulation, with this sole difference, that the force of gravity in the apparatus acts the same part almost exactly that the elasticity of the arteries does in the blood-vessels. When the pump P begins to act it draws in the liquid by aspiration, and then propels it upward through the tube T, so as not only to urge it along but overcome the force of its gravity. But the force thus expended by the pump is not lost, for no sooner is the liquid injected into the funnel than it reacts with the whole force of its gravity, and produces a uniform current through the funnel and along the whole extent of the lamb's gut to the pump again. Just so the heart propels the blood through the larger pulsating arteries, and at the same time overcomes their elasticity; but the force expended for the latter purpose is not lost, for the elasticity of the arteries reacts upon the blood, and so produces a uniform stream both through the small pulseless arteries and along the capillaries and whole extent of the veins.

I shall now explain in what way the pressure of the atmosphere is of use in removing various obstructions to the progress of the blood.

Mass and weight of liquid.—As the veins are much more capacious than the arteries, the blood accumulates within them, and thus becomes a cause of retardation to its own progress, and so physicians have always dreaded venous plethora as occasioning disease and death. To show the efficacy of the pressure of the atmosphere in obviating such obstructions: suppose the funnel, F G (Fig. 4), to have its tubular portion prolonged into a cistern, C, of any width, and of a depth equal

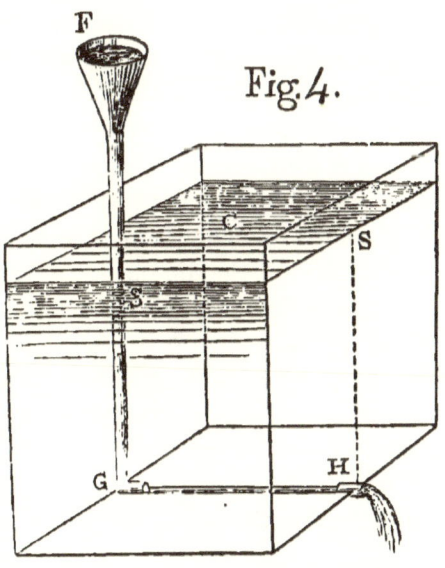

Fig. 4.

to three fourths of the column of liquid, F G. From the orifice G, a grooved channel, open above, crosses the cistern to the aperture, H, into which is inserted a tube of the same size as the tube of the funnel, and opening outwards. Then, if the funnel be kept constantly full, it is manifest that the liquid will at first flow into the cistern with great rapidity, and that comparatively little of it will flow out through the tube, H, so that the liquid will accumulate in the cistern. But just as the liquid accumulates it will flow in more slowly, for the height of the column from F to the surface of the liquid is continually diminishing, and it will flow out more rapidly since the height of the column from H to the surface of the liquid is continually increasing. These changes will go on till the influx and efflux are equal, and at that rate they will continue permanent. Now, it is clear that this will happen when the liquid in the cistern has risen to the point, S, for the column, H S, which regulates the efflux, has now become equal to F S, which regulates the influx, and is just one half of the original column, F G. If, now, a pump be attached to the tube, H, and made to act, the whole liquid accumulated in the cistern will be drawn off; and if the action of the pump be continued thereafter the liquid will never arise above the level of the channel G H. The flow of liquid through the cistern will, therefore, be effected under the pressure of the whole column of liquid, F G, instead of the half of it, F S. That is, the action of the pump will increase the moving force from 1 to 1·4142; or, if a circular movement be given to the liquid, the times of complete revolution, with and without the pump, will be as 1 to 1·4142.

It must here be remarked that the liquid which accumulates in the cistern is intended to denote the venous blood accumulating in the veins; for, if the liquid were surrounded by a membranous envelope sufficiently capacious, it would accumulate and be acted on by the weight of the atmosphere, according to the very same laws, and, therefore, to simplify the problem, the membranous envelope has been left out of consideration.

Mass of liquid and narrow aperture.—If the tube, H, be narrower than the tube of the funnel, then a larger quantity of liquid accumulates before the influx and efflux become equal;

for, when that takes place, F S, the line from F to the surface of the liquid, must be to S H, the line from the surface of the liquid to H, as the diameter of H, the smaller tube, is to the diameter of the larger tube. Thus, if the tube, H, be only in area a ninth part of the tube of the funnel, the cistern will be quite full before the efflux becomes equal to the influx; for we then have F S is to S H as 1 to 3. In this case, the use of the pump would double the quantity of liquid discharged in a given time, and make a circular movement be performed in half the time.

Obstruction from capillary tubes.—Of the mode in which this obstruction is overcome, the caoutchouc pump which I employed furnished of itself an illustration. To prevent any gross particles getting inside and interfering with the action of the valves, the liquid has been made to enter the pump through four apertures in a brass disc not larger than to admit a needle. Now, if such a disc, unconnected with a pump, were bound across the further end of the membranous tube (Fig. 3) the flow of liquid would be greatly impeded; but it would be again expedited by attaching the pump. The same would hold of a disc perforated with many still smaller apertures, which might be compared to capillaries. But if there were only one or two such apertures, then it is manifest with what force the liquid would require to enter to supply the quantity necessary for the working of the pump, and thus the whole weight of the atmosphere might press upon the membranous tube without any risk of giving to the liquid too high a momentum, that is, of transgressing the limits beyond which the pump would cease to act regularly.

Length of membranous tube.—If the circulation were carried on by a propulsive force alone, the length of the column of venous blood to be pressed along would be one of the principal impediments to its progress. Now, the pressure of the atmosphere is signally adapted to remove this impediment; for the longer the tube the less is the risk of any too powerful action of the pump exhausting the liquid in the tube and causing it to collapse. If a pump be made to act upon an expanse of liquid, the part in which the pump is immersed is not exhausted first, for the air presses upon the whole surface of the liquid, and produces everywhere a simultaneous subsidence of level. Now, the very same happens in an elongated tube lying on a plain surface; for in every part of it the liquid subsides simultaneously, so that the part to which the pump is attached is not emptied more than every other part of it.

If the part of the membranous tube to which the pump is attached be raised perpendicularly, a more or less complete collapse appears on working the pump quickly. The propulsive force of course diminishes just as the pump is raised, and ceases altogether when it comes to the upper level of the funnel, but this is not the cause of the collapse that takes place below that point. It is entirely due to the great shortness of the tube, which is now measured at each successive level by the mere diameter of the tube, but if at any level a platform be formed on which a sufficient portion of the tube can be made to rest, the collapse at once disappears.

These illustrations will suffice for our argument. I have not attempted to enumerate all the impediments to the propulsion of the blood, nor to estimate their relative amount, or the total degree of obstruction which they occasion. I shall, however, point out, hereafter, grounds for believing that, immediately after birth, the circulation is mainly carried on by two forces— the propulsive force of the heart and the pressure of the atmosphere, acting nearly in the proportion of three of the former to two of the latter; but that as life advances, and the quantity of venous blood increases, the latter force becomes relatively more powerful.

Having now shown that it is in perfect accordance with the laws of physics to suppose that the weight of the atmosphere pressing upon the external surface of the blood-vessels should be an auxiliary force in carrying on the circulation of the blood, we proceed to point out the pneumatic forces by which this object is effected, the physical principles upon which their action depends, and the physiological phenomena which attest their influence over the circulation of the blood.

THE PNEUMATIC FORCES

SECTION II.—*Pneumatic Forces in the Human Body considered individually*

Pneumatic forces enumerated.—The pneumatic forces we have to consider are those of the chest, of the heart, and of the arteries, and the force of a complex apparatus, to which we give the name of pleuro-cardiac. The forces of the heart and of the arteries are the most widely diffused throughout the animal kingdom. They seem to be modifications and a higher development of the force of the pulsatile vessels, more allied to veins than to arteries, which exist in animals destitute of a heart. The force of the chest exists in its most perfect state in mammalians and birds, in which it is the most powerful auxiliary to the propulsive force of the heart in carrying on the circulation of the blood; and for that reason we shall speak of it in the first place.

I. *Pneumatic force of chest.*—All the pneumatic forces depend on the alternate amplification and contraction of a hollow organ, to the interior cavity of which the blood has free access, and is forced into the enlarging cavity by the pressure of the atmosphere. It is unnecessary to describe the cavity of the chest, or the complicated muscular action by which it is amplified. Nearly the whole venous blood of the body flows into it on its way to the heart—which, with the great veins leading towards it, and the whole blood-vessels of the pulmonary circuit, are situated entirely within the cavity. No doubt could be entertained that when the chest enlarged the blood must be forced into it by the atmospheric pressure, were it not that the chest is not accessible to blood alone, but has also a free communication with the external air which unquestionably rushes into it as soon as it begins to enlarge, and continues to do so till it is fully expanded. What, then, are the physical principles which come into play when a liquid and an aërial fluid have both free access to the same expanding cavity? It is under these conditions that the chest expands in inspiration; but the physical principles involved will be better understood by considering them in the first instance with reference to a more simple pneumatic apparatus.

Dr Arnott's " bloodless experiment" to disprove it.—The apparatus we have first to speak of differs very much from the respiratory apparatus, but we must consider it in order to obviate an objection of Dr Arnott's which he makes specially against the pneumatic agency of the chest, as he did the objection already spoken of against pneumatic agency in all its forms.

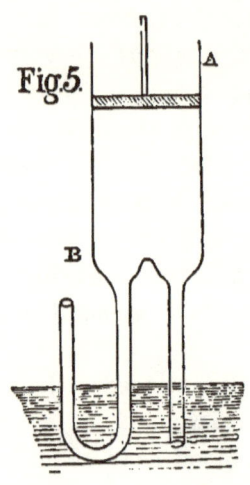

Fig.5.

Let A B be a syringe having two pipes attached to its cylindrical part, by one of which the air has free access, while the other has its lower end immersed in water. On raising the piston slowly, air only will enter the cylinder. But if the piston be raised rapidly, and more especially if the air be impeded in its passage through the air-tube, there will be an agitation of the surface of the water, and a temporary rise of it in the water-tube till the air gradually enters, when the water subsides to its original level.

This is exactly the " bloodless experiment" of Dr Arnott,— so named by him in contradistinction to Barry's sanguinary experiments,—on which he relies to overturn the doctrine of the pneumatic force of the chest; but it is quite beside the mark, having in reality no connection with that doctrine as stated below. If a person hold a glass tube in his mouth while the other end is immersed in water, and then makes an inspiration through the nostrils, it is obvious that the tube and the nostrils correspond to the water and air-pipes in the above apparatus, while the diaphragm plays the part of the piston. The result is exactly the same, depending on the degree of obstruction of the air-tube. " In tranquil breathing with both nostrils, the fluctuation in the tube is," according to Dr Arnott, " less than half an inch either way; with one nostril closed, and the other a little compressed, it may amount to a whole inch; and in convulsive breathing it may exceed twelve inches." Hence, Dr Arnott considers, "that an inch column of blood is the measure of the greatest sugescent power of the chest, and that the heart has to lift a column of blood an inch longer during inspiration and an inch shorter during expiration." I agree fully with Dr Arnott that if the doctrine of the pneumatic power of the chest had no other foundation than this, it should at once be abandoned.

Cavity of chest—divided into pulmonary and circum-pulmonary cavities.—The cavity of the chest, considered as a pneumatic apparatus, is divided into two distinct cavities, separated from each other by the mucous membrane of the lungs. Into one of these cavities air alone enters; while into the other the blood enters, but no air is allowed to penetrate in normal circumstances; and when it does penetrate, from injury or disease, it impedes or arrests the pneumatic operation. As this is a fundamental distinction in our whole argument, I give to these two cavities the names of the pulmonary and circum-pulmonary cavities, corresponding to the air-sac and water-chamber in the typical apparatus described below.

The pulmonary cavity contains air only, and upon inspiration it is blown up like a bladder, which is the simple form of the lung in the serpent tribe; while in the higher animals the bladder is subdivided by dissepiments into smaller cavities, all communicating with each other. But as these subdivisions serve only certain subordinate purposes, the simple bladder shape is the best fitted to illustrate our argument.

The circum-pulmonary cavity intervenes between the ribs and diaphragm on the one hand, and the mucous membrane of the lungs on the other. It is also subdivided, for certain important secondary purposes, into several cavities,—the two cavities of the pleura, the cavity of the pericardium, and the cavity of the heart and blood-vessels. These cavities are separated by pliant membranes, and stand exactly in the same mutual physical relations to the pulmonary cavity. We shall therefore regard them as constituting only a single circum-pulmonary cavity, for whatever can be proved of the general cavity can be proved also of any of its subdivisions individually.

Typical apparatus, or respiratory pump; divided like chest into air-sac and water-chamber. — We modify our apparatus in conformity with the description just given, in order to illustrate the physical conditions under which, on the amplification of the thorax, air rushes into the pulmonary cavity, and blood simultaneously into the circum-pulmonary cavity. We represent (Figs. 6 and 9), therefore, the cavity of the thorax or chest by a glass vessel which admits of being amplified and again contracted by a piston or diaphragm. The interior of the vessel is divided into two parts by an elastic membrane in the form of a sac with an exterior opening, through which the air rushes and distends the sac on raising the piston. This air-sac corresponds to the pulmonary cavity. The other division of the vessel, or water-chamber, corresponds to the circum-pulmonary cavity. It is prolonged downward (Fig. 6), horizontally (Fig. 9), or upward, and terminates in a vessel of water by an open orifice, through which the water enters on raising the piston.

We have thus reduced the problem to be solved to its simplest terms, and we have now to inquire what are the physical laws which the air and water must obey on alternately elevating and depressing the piston.

In the first place, it is obvious that if the water-tube be stopped by a cork, and the piston be alternately raised and depressed, we have then an exact representation of the play of the lungs; for the air-sac is gradually distended as the piston ascends, and collapses as it descends. There is, indeed, this difference, that the surface of the lungs is always in immediate contact with the walls of the chest,—while in our apparatus there is some air between the sac and the sides of the cylinder; but this serves to render the movements of the parts more conspicuous, and in no way interferes with the accuracy of the representation. We have, indeed, only to suppose the intervening air to be a light, solid substance, perfectly elastic, and so pliant as to adapt itself to the altering shape of the cavity, and we have the surface of the air-sac in immediate contact with this substance, just as the surface of the lungs is in contact with the expanding walls of the chest.

Pump destitute of valves; draws in water but does not expel it.—If now the water-tube be left open, the apparatus becomes a pump of a peculiar structure, admirably adapted to the purposes it is intended to serve in the living economy. In the first place, it has no valves, which are essential to the operation of a common pump. But it is obvious that the interposition of valves where the great veins enter the chest would have been disadvantageous to the circulation; for whenever these valves were shut, they would have been a barrier to the current of venous blood, destroying whatever power that current has in dilating the cavities of the right side of the heart; just as the valves upon the right side of the heart destroy that power altogether, and so prevent the influence it would otherwise have in filling the pulmonary vessels. In the second place, the respiratory pump (as I shall name it), while it draws in liquid to its cavity during the ascent of the piston, does not expel it during the descent of the piston,—the expulsive force telling solely upon the air in the air-sac, and not affecting the liquid in the water-chamber. A common pump, deprived of its valves, becomes a mere syringe, in which, whatever quantity of liquid be drawn in during the ascent of the piston, it is again expelled as the piston descends. The peculiarity of our apparatus is, that although destitute of valves, and drawing in liquid like a syringe during the ascent of the piston, it does not, if properly worked, expel the liquid as the piston descends. Just so the act of inspiration draws blood into the chest, while the act of expiration, in all ordinary circumstances, has no power to expel it. This obviates what has always been considered the most formidable objection to the pneumatic agency of the chest upon the circulating blood.

Action depends on elasticity, weight, and position of membrane of sac.—The peculiar action of the respiratory pump, to which it owes its utility, depends upon the properties of the membrane forming the air-sac,—that is to say, surrounding the pulmonary cavity and separating it from the circum-pulmonary. These properties are of two kinds. In the first place, it must oppose a certain resistance to the entrance of the air by which the sac is distended; for that resistance is at once the source and the exact measure of the force with which the liquid is drawn into the water-chamber or circum-pulmonary cavity.

In the second place, the membrane forming the sac must have an inherent power of emptying the sac of the air by which it has been distended as soon as the distending force ceases to act, and without the assistance of any extrinsic force. By an inherent power of the membrane, I mean a power depending upon its inherent properties; and of these I know only two to which such an expulsive power could be referred, viz., elasticity and gravity assisted by a fitting position of the sac.

When a caoutchouc bag is inflated, if the orifice by which the air has been blown in is not immediately stopped, the elasticity of the bag immediately expels the air, at first with great force, and then with a force gradually decreasing till the bag is nearly empty. Now, the tissues of the lungs, or those forming the trachea, the bronchial tubes, and the pulmonary cells, are all of them eminently elastic, and are therefore fitted, when the lungs have been inflated, to expel the air from them without the aid of any extrinsic force; that is to say, by their own inherent power, just like the membrane of a caoutchouc bag in similar circumstances.

Provision of nature to augment elasticity.—Here it is impossible not to advert to two beautiful arrangements by which nature intensifies this elastic force of the lungs, so as to avail herself of it to the highest possible degree. The first is, that the lungs in ordinary breathing only expel one eighth part of their total contents. Now, just as in the caoutchouc bag, the elasticity of the lungs is greatest when the first portion of the air is expelled from them, and would have become gradually weaker had the expulsion proceeded farther. The second arrangement is the great extent given to the elastic tissue of the lungs by the multiplication of cells and minute cylinders, instead of a simple sac, as in the serpent. Now, the elasticity is in proportion to the extent of the elastic tissue. One thousand pulmonary cells have ten times more extent of tissue, and ten times more expulsive force, than a single sac having the same cubic content.

When the air-sac is formed of a thick, dense tissue, like that of a foot-ball, if the sac be properly placed, with the orifice downmost, the weight of the sac will co-operate with its elasticity in expelling the air after inflation; while, in less favorable positions, the weight of the sac might be a great impediment to the expulsion of the air. This was at first a difficulty in constructing a working model of the respiratory pump; but the most essential condition to be observed is to follow nature in not permitting the expulsion of the air to be carried too far, but restricting the quantity of air expelled at each respiration to a small fraction of the whole amount, as explained above. The weight of the lungs, from the vast network of blood-vessels they contain, and the quantity of blood contained in them, must be very considerable; but, in whatever position the body is placed—upright, supine, prone, or on the side—it seems to contribute to the expulsion of the inhaled air.

To resume, then:—The utility and special action of our apparatus depend mainly on the properties of the membrane forming the air-sac, in virtue of which it first opposes the entrance of air into the sac, and again immediately expels it on the distending force ceasing to operate. To explain its mode of action in detail, we must consider separately three different cases; in which the action of the apparatus varies according as the water enters the water-chamber from the same level, or from a higher or a lower level.

Action of pump modified by level of inhaled water.—The blood entering the chest may be considered as virtually, in all normal circumstances, coming from a higher level of about nine inches; for we have found a column of blood of that height to be the measure of the force of the heart remaining at the end of the jugular vein, and we have found that such a force is indispensable to the action of a pneumatic force on flaccescent tubes. The only use of a pump in such circumstances must be to accelerate the entrance of the blood. If, again, the liquid were to come from the same level, which would be nearly the case in the veins without and within the chest, if we made no account of the remaining impulse derived from the heart, and as actually occurs when the force of the heart is very feeble, or arrested in a fainting fit—then the liquid would have no tendency

4

to enter but for the action of the pump. In neither of these cases would the descent of the piston be followed by any retrogressive movement of the inhaled liquid. But, on the contrary, if the liquid comes from a lower level, while it is drawn in during the ascent of the piston, it flows out during the descent— not from any force exerted by the piston, but simply from its own gravity. This case, although resembling least what occurs in nature, we shall nevertheless consider chiefly as being best adapted to illustrate the physical action of the apparatus, and still more as supplying us with an accurate measure of the inhaling power of the apparatus at every stage of the dilatation of the sac.

Water from below—Vertical tube of uniform diameter.—When

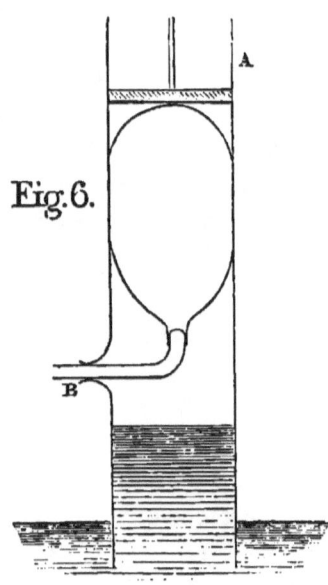

Fig. 6.

the liquid enters the instrument from a lower level, the phenomena which present themselves on working the piston are different according as the water-chamber has the form of a tube of uniform area (Fig. 6), or has a wider area above than at the orifice (Figs. 7, 8). To take first the simpler case, in which the water-tube is of uniform area (Fig. 6) :—On elevating the piston, not only will the air-sac be distended, but the water will rise in the water-tube to a definite level, at which it will remain as long as the piston is kept elevated.

The explanation of these phenomena is simple. The air no longer rushes into the sac with the same force with which it rushed into the empty syringe (Fig. 5); for a certain part of the force has to be expended in distending the sac. It is manifest that when the sac is in a state of collapse, a certain force is required to overcome its elasticity if it have any, or at all events its inertia by which it resists distension. But on raising

the piston the water is forced into the tube with the whole force
of the atmosphere, and it must rise in the tube till equilibrium
be produced, and that will obviously happen when the weight
of the column of water is just equal to the resistency of the air-
sac. This is manifest from considering that the elasticity of
the air included in the cylinder together with the resistency of
the bladder is just equal to the atmospheric pressure; and the
elasticity of the included air together with the weight of the
column of water in the water-tube is also equal to the atmospheric pressure. Whence on equal areas the resistency of the
bladder or elastic sac is just equal to the weight of the column
of water in the water-tube. If, for instance, the included air
were rarefied to one half, and the apparatus were sufficiently
capacious, then the water in the water-tube would stand at the
height of 16 feet, and the force with which every square inch of
the sac resisted further distension would be equal to $7\frac{1}{4}$ pounds.

It may be here remarked that we could in this way measure
the resistency of the lungs; which must depend partly on the
elasticity of the pulmonary tissues, but a great deal also on mere
inertia, since the pulmonary vessels filled with blood are ramified
upon the surface and throughout the substance of the lungs.

Lastly, when the piston descends, the column of water falls
in the water-tube, just as the sac is emptied of air by its own
expulsive power; the height of the diminishing column of water
being always an exact index of the degree of resistency of the sac.

It is worthy of remark, as illustrating more fully the principles on which the instrument works, that if instead of a piston,
which always occasions a certain amount of resistance from
friction, we employ a diaphragm, then no sooner does the hand
bearing up the diaphragm let go its hold than the diaphragm
spontaneously descends, for the pressure of the atmospheric air
above it is greater than that of the rarefied air in the cylinder
supporting it below. But no sooner is the equilibrium dis-
turbed between the air in the cylinder and that in the air-sac,
than the elasticity and weight of the membrane of the sac comes
into play, and expels the air which it contains, and all this goes
on till the air in the cylinder at length becomes of the same
density as the external air, when equilibrium is again re-estab-

lished as at first. The diaphragm is now again raised, and the
air-sac is filled ; on removing the hand it is again emptied without the aid of any extrinsic force, so that the air within the
cylinder never becomes more dense than that without, and
can never therefore exert any expulsive force upon any liquid
that may have entered it from the same or from a higher level.

Vertical tube wider above than below.—Let us now consider
the second case (Figs. 7, 8), in which the vertical tube is wider
above than below.` When the water-tube is of uniform area
there is complete harmony in the movements of the air and the
water, both during the ascent and the descent of the piston ;
the air rushes into and is again expelled from the air-sac just
as the water rises and falls in the water-tube, for the weight
of the column of water always keeps equal to the resistency of
the sac. But this harmony is at once destroyed if we make
use of a tube which is wider above than it is below, and the
effect is, if we may so speak, to give to the water complete
precedence over the air.

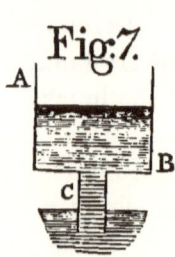

Let the tube A B C become at the point
B thrice or any number of times greater in diameter, so that the upper half of it has nine times
the area of the lower. Then, other arrangements as before, when the piston is raised the
water will rise in the lower part of the tube, as
explained above ; but as soon as it reaches the
upper and wider part of the tube its progress
upward is retarded, for it rises in the upper part of the tube
nine times more slowly than in the lower. But we have seen
that the dilatation of the air-sac goes on *pari passu* with the
rise of the liquid in the lower tube, and therefore nine times
faster than the rise of the liquid in the enlarged tube. Hence
the air-sac is rapidly distended to the uttermost. But there is
here no equilibrium, and such a state of matters cannot last,
seeing there is an inequality between the column of water and
the resistency of the air-sac, and there only can be equilibrium
when each of these, added to the elasticity of the air included
in the cylinder, is equal to the pressure of the external air.
The consequence is, that if the piston be kept elevated the

Fig. 7.
A
B
C

water slowly rises in the water-tube, and the air-sac slowly contracts until at length equilibrium is produced; and the water will only attain its full height, corresponding to the full distension of the sac, after several short movements of the piston upward.

The effect of the descent of the piston is equally remarkable. The contraction of the air-sac goes on with the same rapidity with which the water would have descended in a tube of uniform area; but in the wide tube it descends nine times more slowly. Hence the air-sac rapidly collapses, while a large proportion of the water is still within the large part of the tube; and if the piston continues in constant motion upward and downward, in accordance with the state of the air-sac alone, so long will the water remain included in the larger tube oscillating upward and downward within limits which are determined by the rapidity of the movement of the piston.

If, after the collapse of the air-sac, the piston were forced still farther downward, the whole of the water, both in the large and in the small tube, would be expelled, and on again raising the piston the same series of phenomena would be repeated from the beginning. But if, after the water has once accumulated within the tube, the motion of the piston be limited, like that of the ribs and diaphragm in expiration, to the mere expulsion of a small proportion of the air from the sac, then will the liquid remain permanently accumulated within the tube.

It is obvious that the greater the increase of area of the wider part of the tube, the greater will be the accumulation of

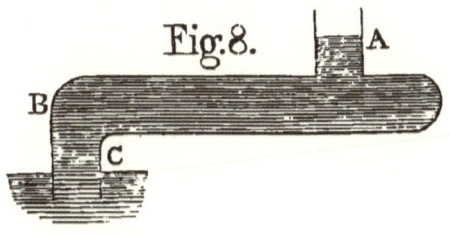

Fig. 8.

liquid; and if the cylinder, instead of being vertical, be placed horizontally, then the length of the horizontal part of the

cylinder may be made to represent the increase of area, and the accumulation within the cylinder will be proportionally great.

Water from same level.—We have hitherto supposed the level of the water inhaled to be below the water-chamber; but if the water-chamber and the water to be inhaled are on the same horizontal level (Fig. 9), as is literally the case with the chest when we are recumbent, in respect to the great veins penetrating into it, then it is obvious, first, that the force of gravity is no longer an obstacle to the influx of liquid into the water-chamber; and second, that when the force which caused at once the dilatation of the air-sac and the influx of water

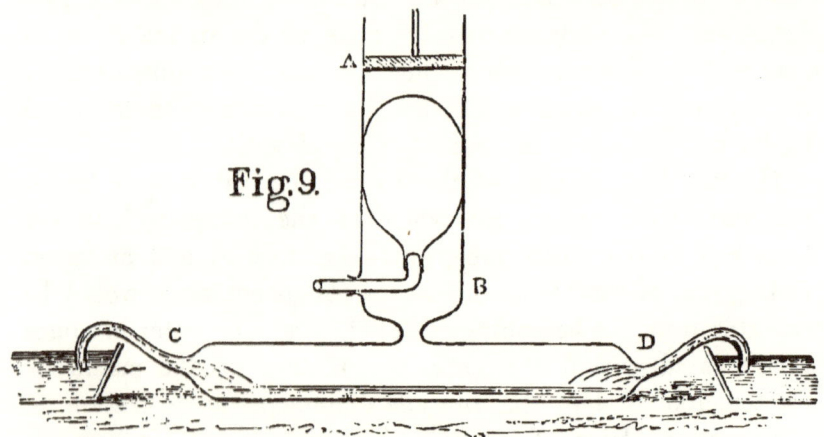

Fig. 9.

ceases to operate, then the air alone will be expelled by the spontaneous contraction of the air-sac, while there is not the slightest retrogressive movement of the inhaled water. Gravity was the sole cause of the efflux of the water from the vertical tube, but that cause no longer operates at a horizontal level. It is exactly in this way that air alone is expelled from the lungs by an ordinary expiration, without any refluent movement of the blood. Farther, if the influent liquid, instead of being allowed to spread itself freely throughout the horizontal chamber C D, be received into a bit of gut, or large vein, it will distend the gut or vein as it flows in, just as the influent blood does the venæ cavæ during inspiration.

Water from above.—Lastly, if the inhaled water, instead of coming from a vessel on the same level as the water-chamber, come from a vessel placed 9·45 inches above it, then upon raising the piston will the water be forced into the water-chamber, not merely by the pressure of the atmosphere, but also by the pressure of a column of water 9·45 inches in height. Exactly in this way is the blood upon inspiration forced into the venæ cavæ and cavities of the right side of the heart, not only by the pressure of the atmosphere, but by the pressure of a column of blood of the weight just indicated. This same force would distend also the pulmonary vessels, both arteries and veins, and the cavities of the left side of the heart, did not the valves and contraction of the right side of the heart form a complete barrier to its further extension.

It is scarcely necessary to repeat that the whole phenomena we have described as taking place in rigid tubes would take place also in veins or other flaccessent tubes under the pressure of a column of liquid of the height just mentioned, or under the influence of an equivalent vis a tergo or propulsive force from behind.

Action of typical apparatus compared with that of chest.— To conclude this part of our argument. The very same principles of physics which regulate the entrance and expulsion of air and liquid in the simple apparatus we have been describing, regulate also the entrance and expulsion of air and liquid in the cavity of the chest. To speak more precisely, the movement of the piston denotes the movement of the diaphragm and ribs; the air-sac represents the pulmonary cavity, or that bounded by the mucous membrane of the lungs; the water-chamber corresponds to the whole space which we have named the circum-pulmonary cavity, or that intervening between the lungs and the parietes of the chest, together with the medias-tinum or space intervening between the lungs, and stretching the whole length of the thorax from the spine to the breast-bone. The anatomist, deriving his ideas from the dead body as he sees it on dissection, speaks of the two cavities of the pleura, and that of the pericardium ; but such cavities are unknown in the living body, for both the lungs and the heart have a serous membrane surrounding and in immediate contact with them to facilitate their movements by the secretion with which they are lubricated. The only part of the circum-pulmonary space which is accessible to blood consists of the great systemic veins, the cavities of the right side of the heart, the pulmonary vessels, both arteries and veins, and the cavities of the left side of the heart. At birth, and for a brief period thereafter, the whole of this irregular and far-stretching cavity is not only accessible to blood, but has the blood forced into it by the pressure of the atmosphere; but in the adult, as has been shown above, the right side of the heart forms a barrier to the atmospheric pressure, which does not extend therefore to the pulmonary vessels and left cavities of the heart. The blood rushes into and distends the veins and the right side of the heart upon the descent of the diaphragm and expansion of the ribs at the very same time, and from the same cause that the air rushes into and distends the lungs. The entrance of the blood and of the air into the chest is due to the very same physical laws, according to which, on raising the piston in the respiratory pump, the air rushes into and distends the air-sac, and the water rushes into the water-chamber. When, again, the inspiratory effort ceases, and the chest returns to its former size, the air is at once expelled by the physical contraction of the tissue of the lungs, and of the parietes of the thorax and parts around it; but there is no expulsion of the inhaled blood which remains permanently within the chest, providing a plentiful supply for the gaping cavities of the heart. Not otherwise in our apparatus, when the piston, on the cessation of the elevating force, is allowed to descend, the air-sac expels the air by its own contractile power; but there is no retro-gressive movement of the water in the water-chamber. Lastly, both in the natural and artificial apparatus, the retention of the liquid within the cavity is effected without the aid of valves, which, had they been placed at the entrance of the great veins into the chest, would have formed an obstacle to the propulsive force of the left ventricle extending into the chest, and required there constantly to assist in the distension of the right cavities of the heart.

Diagrams and working model.—With respect to the *Figures*

in various places accompanying the text, it is proper to state that only one of them (Fig. 3) represents an apparatus actually constructed and practically tested, so that the propositions it is intended to prove rest on experimental evidence. All the rest are mere diagrams like the figures accompanying the propositions in a mathematical work, and answering a similar end, for they are all intended to represent to the eye the physical conditions under consideration, and so indicate them to the mind with more precision than mere words could effect. The propositions themselves were originally drawn up in the old style of Borelli, but when I began to think of making them public I felt that such a mode of treating the subject was altogether abhorrent from the taste of the present day, and I therefore gave to them a lighter form. But this does not in any way alter the nature of the evidence on which they rest, which is purely demonstrative, though without the formality of reference to acknowledged principles. To those who have the patience to study them as mere physico-mathematical theorems they will give an assurance of certainty to the conclusions deduced from them which no other evidence could impart.

But it is always desirable to confirm theoretical deductions by experiment, and there are many men to whose minds the evidence of experiment is more conclusive than any other. I have therefore been at much pains in devising a working model of the "Respiratory Pump," as I name the apparatus by which the respiration and circulation of the blood are simultaneously maintained, and have taken advantage, in the construction of it, of most of the principles indicated above. Inspiration is effected by a diaphragm working upward in a large glass cylinder. Expiration takes place by the spontaneous descent of the diaphragm. The elastic air-sac can be so adjusted as to expel at every respiration only a small portion of its total contents, and so keep up its elastic force at the highest rate. The sac is placed vertically, and opens downwards, so as to make the forces of gravity and elasticity co-operate in expelling the air from the sac. Advantage has also been taken of the harmony with which the elastic air-sac and a vertical water-

tube of uniform diameter work together ; and both are introduced into the apparatus, as the latter does not interfere with
the action of the former, and gives the great advantage of
allowing the inhaled liquid to run off by gravity, and so
preventing its accumulation in the water-chamber. In this
way a continuous current through the apparatus is maintained,
the liquid rushing in at each inspiration never exhibiting any
retrogressive tendency during expiration, and being discharged
solely by its own weight.*

II. *Pneumatic force of the heart and of the arteries.*—The physical principles on which the pneumatic force of the heart and of
the arteries depends, are exactly the same as those by means of
which we fill with water a caoutchouc bag having a tubulated
aperture, by merely immersing the nozzle of the tube in the
liquid, after having compressed the bag with the hand, so as to
expel the air contained in it. Exactly in the same way, by the
alternate contraction and relaxation of the hand, we work the
various kinds of injecting apparatus, which in their mechanism
exactly resemble the ventricles of the heart, as they consist of
a bag of elastic tissue which contracts by the muscular force of
the hand, and then returns to its former size, in virtue of
its elasticity, as soon as the pressure is intermitted,—while it is
provided with two valves to direct the current of the liquid, one
of them opening inward, and so resembling the auriculo-ventricular valves, and the other opening outward like the sigmoid
valves at the root of the great arterial trunks.

It is manifest that a pneumatic force such as we have
described must exist necessarily, and operate in every hollow
organ filled and freely supplied with liquid, in which a
muscular and elastic tissue are combined together and antago-
nise each other, provided the apparatus be subject to the
pressure of the atmosphere. It only remains, therefore, to
inquire whether this is the structure of the heart and of the
arteries.

That such is the structure of the arteries is known certainly ;

* The apparatus described above was constructed for me by Mr J. White,
78, Union Street, Philosophical Instrument Maker to the University of Glasgow,
who has kindly consented to show it in operation to those curious in such matters.

and there can therefore be no doubt that the atmospheric pressure assists in keeping the arteries full of blood when they expand, after having been contracted by their muscular power ; but we have already seen that there is no provision of valves, nor any rhythmic succession of movements, by which the muscular power of the arteries could be rendered effective in carrying on the circulation of the blood.

As to the heart, it seems to me impossible to deduce the existence of any expansive force resident in its walls from the recognised properties of the tissues of which they consist, as we see them after death,—and it is an improbable hypothesis that the heart possesses during life an elasticity which no other muscular tissue is known to be endowed with. How, then, are we to explain the unequivocal indications which the heart of a living animal exhibits of spontaneous dilatation? The heart of an animal tenacious of life beats, often for whole days, after being separated from the body, constantly resuming its natural shape in the intervals between the contractions. Every one who has witnessed the action of the heart in a living animal, and laid hold of it, must have been struck with the great distension of its cavities, which swell out firmly in the hand that supports them. Haller and Magendie both declare that it is impossible to prevent the dilatation of the heart, even of a small animal, by the pressure of both hands.

It appears to me most probable that the expansive power of the heart resides, not in its walls, but in the transverse septum which separates the auricles from the ventricles and gives to the organ its contour at its thickest part. This septum, usually called the base of the ventricles, is made up of fibrous and fibro-cartilaginous tissue intermixed with muscular fibres. It exhibits four apertures, the two inlets and the two outlets of the ventricles,—usually called the auriculo-ventricular and arterial orifices. These apertures are always patent when the heart is quiescent, as we see it after death. The two inlets are never more distended, but admit of complete contraction ; the two outlets are never more contracted, but admit of farther distension. The whole four exhibit constant movements which are exactly synchronous, but the inlets and outlets are in a state of complete antagonism, the one shutting and remaining shut at the exact time when the other opens and remains open. The same mechanism, indeed, to a certain extent, produces these opposite effects. Thus, the inlets are shut by the contracting fibres of the ventricles just at the moment when the stream of blood issuing from the ventricles distends the outlets. But the most interesting of the whole phenomena is the immediate starting open of the two inlets, or auriculo-ventricular orifices, as soon as the relaxing fibres of the ventricles cease to retain them. This seems to be due to the whole transverse septum resuming its ordinary diameter and shape, after being condensed and bent downwards at the circumference by the force of the ventricles in their contraction. But the opening of the auriculo-ventricular orifice extends the base of the ventricle, and so gives a corresponding widening to the whole conical cavity. The consequence is that the blood, which has always free access to the auricles, and with which the auricles are now distended, makes its way into the ventricles also and distends them, not only with a like force, which we have found upon the right side to be equal to 5·453 oz. upon every square inch of surface, but also with whatever force may result from the active dilatation of the auriculo-ventricular orifices.

The apparatus attached to the inlet of the ventricles, and usually named the "auriculo-ventricular valves," has a totally different structure from the sigmoid valves, or any other valves, whether in the sanguiferous or the lymphatic system. All of these valves have a free margin, and are shut by the mere force of the refluent liquid. In this apparatus alone the free margin of the tendinous expansion surrounding the inlet is tied down by tendinous cords to the inner surface of the ventricle, in such a manner as to prevent all movement of it backwards when the cords are on the stretch; and by pulling them firmly downwards they shut the inlet, acting exactly like purse-strings in shutting the mouth of a purse. The whole apparatus, comprehending the tendinous membrane, the cords, and the projecting fleshy columns to which the cords are attached, appears to me to constitute a sphincter, intended for the complete occlusion of the aperture between the auricles and the ventricles; and to work most probably in the following way. The aperture, which is wide open when the auricles are full, is gradually narrowed during the contraction of the auricles, and reduced to a very small size as the last portion of blood is forced through it into the ventricle. The tendon is now in the most favorable position to admit of the lengthening of its tendinous cords, which are drawn downward by the elongation of the distended ventricle. But no sooner does the ventricle begin to contract than the tendinous cords are more forcibly stretched by the shortening of the fleshy columns, from the ends of which they arise. The whole tendon is thus drawn downward, and the aperture closed and maintained in the state of occlusion till the end of the systole. No sooner, however, do the muscular fibres of the ventricle cease to act, than the tendinous cords are relaxed, and the elasticity of the sides of the aperture restore it from the constrained position into which it had been drawn to its original patency.

The action of the tendinous cords, in shutting the aperture, is well seen in the heart of the ox, by opening the left ventricle from below, and passing a string all round between the tendinous cords and the walls of the ventricle. Upon now pulling the string downward, the whole cords are simultaneously stretched, and on looking to the ventricle from above, the orifice will be seen accurately closed, the tendinous membrane adapting itself thereto by numerous folds, with intervening digitations, exactly resembling the folds and projecting digitations of the skin around any other sphincter in a state of occlusion. This is much better seen in the circular aperture on the left side than in the elongated and less regular opening upon the right.

It may be farther argued that the diminution of the transverse diameter of the heart, which takes place during the systole, as it cannot be owing to the state of the outlets which are then fully distended, must be referred to the collapse of the inlets.

Neither is the valve hypothesis without its difficulties. In Fig. 229, 'Quain's Anatomy,' (vol. i, p. 305), the valves are

shown with the segments distended as they are believed to be
during the systole. Each of the orifices is expanded to the
uttermost, with the valve like a ship under sail coming through
into the auricle, and only prevented from doing so by the
tendinous cords, to which this sole office is assigned. But if
this expanded state of the base of the ventricle continue during
the whole time of the systole, how can the conical cavity be
emptied of its blood, which accumulates in greatest quantity
just at the base?

The whole subject of the action of the heart seems to me to
require revision. It has been regarded too much as the action
of two distinct organs in a state of antagonism to each other,
and not as the rhythmical action of a single organ,—the several
parts of which assume in succession the states of distension,
contraction, and moderate dilatation, which, after a pause,
passes into distension again. In the simple dorsal vein we see
these changes commence behind, and pass forward through
every part of the vein in succession; and not otherwise, in the
more complex apparatus of the higher animals we have these
same changes occurring first in the great veins entering the
auricle, next in the auricle itself, then probably in the inlet to
the ventricle, next in the ventricle itself, and lastly in the outlet and, where it exists, in the bulbus arteriosus.

III. *Pleuro-cardiac Pneumatic force.*—But the most important
aspect under which we can contemplate the pneumatic action of
the heart is, when we regard the heart as the centre of a
pneumatic system to the dilatative force of which it contributes
nothing, while it regulates the whole working of the system
within the limits which the dilatative force will permit. An idea
of such a system will at once be formed if we suppose the air to
be extracted from a pericardium made of glass, and the heart to
be supplied by rigid tubes with blood subject to the atmospheric
pressure. Then, every time the heart contracted in the vacuum
of the pericardium, its cavities would be again distended forcibly by the blood impelled into it by the atmospheric pressure, and the oftener the heart contracted, the more blood
would be forced into it and again expelled, the only limits
being those determined by the degree of exhaustion of the air

in the pericardium and the working capabilities of the mechanism of the heart.

Such, virtually, is the position of the right side of the heart in the circum-pulmonary cavity; for after every contraction of the right auricle and ventricle, the blood is impelled into them by the atmospheric pressure, and distends their internal surface with a force greater than that to which their external surface or that looking towards the lungs is subjected. This will be best seen by referring to our typical apparatus (Fig. 10), where

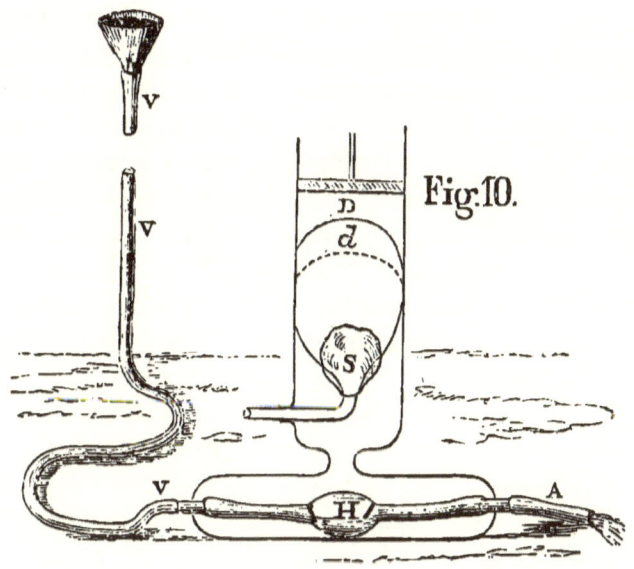

Fig. 10.

V, V, V represent a vein nine inches in height, and kept constantly full, or of which the blood has a corresponding propulsive force. Varying its direction, the vein enters the circum-pulmonary cavity and expands at H into a single pulsating ventricle like that of a crustacean, from which issues an arterial trunk A, which passes out of the circum-pulmonary cavity and discharges its blood. When the air-sac S is undistended, the air in the sac and that in the circum-pulmonary cavity have the same tension—that of the external air; and if the heart were now to act, the blood would be urged into it solely by its own propulsive force and whatever expansive force the heart may possess. But on fully raising the piston the sac is dis-

tended to D, and the air in the circum-pulmonary cavity
becomes less dense than the external air or that in the air-sac.
The consequence is that, in addition to the forces just mentioned, the blood is urged into the heart with a force equal to
the difference between the pressure upon its internal and
external surfaces, or between the tension of the external air
and that contained in the circum-pulmonary cavity. But after
an ordinary expiration, the air-sac does not return to its
original size S, when there would be again equilibrium in the
air within and without the circum-pulmonary cavity. The sac
is only emptied by one eighth as it descends from D to d, so
that there is still inequality of pressure between the two sides of
the heart. In this way the blood, after an ordinary expiration,
instead of being forced backward out of the chest as has been
commonly thought, is still impelled into it at every emptying
of the cavities of the right side of the heart. By this admirable arrangement the pneumatic force of the chest, which of
itself could act only during inspiration, is converted into a
constantly acting force, drawing the blood inward at every beat
of the heart, and in greater quantity the more rapidly the heart
beats. The only difference the respiration occasions being to
make the rush of blood into the heart somewhat greater or less
as the lungs are more or less distended with air.

These remarks apply only to the right side of the heart. It
is true that the left side of the heart and the whole pulmonary
blood-vessels form part of the circum-pulmonary cavity. But
in the adult they are quite secluded from all pressure of the
external air by the barrier which the right side of the heart
interposes. On the left side, therefore, the heart is dilated
solely by its own expansive power, and by the stream of blood
projected from the right ventricle. The aid of a pneumatic
force situated on the right side and signally diminishing the
resistance of the blood in the systemic vessels is given to the
left ventricle alone, which stands most in need of it from the
more arduous labour it has to perform.

THE PNEUMATIC FORCES

SECTION III.—*Physiological Phenomena by which the Influence of Pneumatic Forces in the Living Body is attested.*

While the foundation of the doctrine of pneumatic forces must consist in a demonstration of the physical principles on which they rest, a still more interesting and equally convincing part of our argument consists in pointing out and explaining the numerous physiological phenomena which attest the influence of these pneumatic forces operating within the living body.

The phenomena here in question are peculiar conditions of the circulation, indicating the operation of a pneumatic force; some of them indefinitely, merely pointing to the existence of such a force at or near the centre of the circulation, while others are manifestly connected with the act of respiration.

Without pretending to give a complete analysis of these phenomena, I shall advert to and endeavour to explain some of the most striking, and in doing so I shall adopt the twofold division of them indicated above, beginning with the latter as the most remarkable.

I.—*Pneumatic Phenomena referable to the act of Respiration.*

Inspiration and expiration—effects of, on the veins, arteries, and capillaries.—The changes produced on the whole vascular system by the act of respiration are of the most remarkable kind, and serve strikingly to illustrate and confirm the explanation here adopted of them.

When any of the great veins which enter the chest—the sub-clavian, the jugular, or the inferior cava—are exposed to view in a living animal, they are seen at every inspiration to shrink in size, losing their cylindrical shape, becoming flattened, and as if so far emptied of their blood as to be no longer distended. This change takes place just at the same moment that the external air begins to enter the mouth and nostrils, and continues exactly the same time as the inhalation of the

5

air; moreover, it is the more conspicuous and extended the deeper the inspiration—that is, the more air that enters the lungs, so that it is impossible not to refer to a common cause the shrinking of the veins and the entrance of air into the lungs; and as it is certainly known that the latter depends upon the elasticity of the external air, which is just the same as its pressure, so we infer that it is the pressure of the external air that empties the great veins of their blood, and forces it into the chest.

At every expiration again, or rather interval between the end of one inspiration and the beginning of another, the veins swell out and resume their rotundity; and as these are phenomena the very opposite of those attending inspiration, it has been erroneously inferred, that they proceed from the very opposite cause, the blood being supposed to be forced backward into the veins by the compression of the chest in expiration. We have seen that the blood within the chest undergoes no compression during expiration, and that having once entered the circumpulmonary cavity it cannot again flow out, as it is retained there on somewhat the same principle as water is retained in a bird-fount, the pressure upon it within the chest being less than the pressure of the external air. The true cause of the swelling of the veins during expiration is that after the termination of an inspiration, no more blood, or very little, enters the chest till the beginning of the next inspiration, and the consequence is that the blood propelled onward by the force of the heart accumulates in the veins near the chest to an extent proportionate to the length of the interval.

The changes described above are not confined to the great veins penetrating into the chest, but are visible, though less conspicuous, in all their larger branches, more especially on deep inspiration. In the smaller veins, again, no such changes can be perceived by the eye, but it does not follow that they do not really take place: as must be obvious from considering how rapidly the aggregate area of the veins increases as they recede from the heart; and that at every point the dilatation and contraction of the area of each vein is inversely as the aggregate area; and still farther, that it is only the change in the diameter of a vein that is visible to the eye, and that the diameter is as the square root of the area. Whence the visible contraction and dilatation of the veins at every point is inversely as the square root of the aggregate area of the veins at that point, and this rapidly decreasing ratio must soon render these changes in the veins altogether imperceptible. We are here therefore obliged to part company with M Magendie and the physiologists of his school, who, relying solely on their experiments made upon living animals, maintain that the aspirative power of the chest over the blood extends no farther than the veins which visibly diminish in size during deep inspiration. In opposition to that view we would appeal to purely physical experiments, of which the conditions can be rigorously determined. Such is the experiment detailed above in which the aspirative power of a caoutchouc bag extended over the whole of a piece of lamb's gut, twelve feet in length, as it would have done had the gut been ten times or any number of times longer. Another experiment bearing equally on this subject is that in which the liquid was sucked without impediment through capillary apertures in a brass disc. Such experiments as these remove all difficulties from our path in adopting the opinion that the aspirative power of the chest extends over the whole sanguiferous system—veins, capillaries and arteries; and physiological evidences are not wanting in support of it.

The arteries are affected by the act of respiration as well as the veins, but it is not indicated in the same way. There is no visible shrinking of the arteries during inspiration, or expansion of them during expiration and the period of repose. But changes in the interior of an artery, of which the eye cannot inform us, are discriminated by the touch. Thus the blood injected into the radial artery by each stroke of the left ventricle of the heart occasions no visible augmentation of its diameter, but communicates to the finger the very distinct sensation which we denominate the arterial pulse. Now, according to the united testimony of all physiologists, the pulse is less voluminous and feebler during inspiration, and recovers its volume and strength during expiration and the period of repose.

To explain these changes of the pulse it has been supposed

that the blood is forced backward from the arteries into the chest by the pressure of the atmosphere during inspiration, so making the pulse weaker; while the compression of the chest forces the blood out, and so renders the pulse stronger during expiration. But both these explanations are inadmissible. The reflux of blood along the arteries into the chest is completely prevented by the superior force of the stroke of the heart, assisted by the sigmoid valves and elastic coat of the arteries; and as has been shown above, no compression of the blood in the chest occurs during expiration to give additional strength to the pulse. It is the very same cause which produces the shrinking of the veins and the feeble and small pulse of the arteries during inspiration; for the atmospheric air pressing upon the whole blood-vessels alike, the blood goes in whatever direction there is least resistance; and as all reflux through the arteries is prevented by the propulsive force of the heart and the sigmoid valves, the whole current sets in the opposite direction towards the chest, through the arteries, and from them through the capillaries and veins. The fuller and stronger pulse during expiration and the period of repose is due to the same cause as the refilling of the veins. It is no new or intensive force added to that of the heart, but the mere restoration of the force which had been subducted in inspiration, by the blood then rushing toward the chest, through the veins and arteries alike.

Movements of brain.—Neither can it be objected that there is no evidence from observation to show that there exists in the smaller blood-vessels the alternate emptying and filling which we perceive in the large veins and arteries, and have ascribed on theoretical grounds to the blood-vessels universally. We have explained above how it cannot be seen in any individual small vessel, but in the aggregate blood-vessels pervading the soft substance of the brain we have occasionally opportunities of witnessing it in a most conspicuous form. Cases of injury to the head are to be seen from time to time in all our great hospitals in which a portion of the bones of the cranium having been removed, the brain is exposed to view, sometimes still invested with its fibrous covering (dura mater), but often denuded, and sometimes protruded outwards, constituting the affection named "hernia cerebri." In all such cases we see an alternate movement of the substance of the brain corresponding exactly to the movements of respiration, the brain shrinking and receding into the cranial cavity during inspiration, and again swelling out prominently during expiration and the period of repose. Now, it cannot be doubted that this alternate movement proceeds from the emptying and refilling of the blood-vessels of the brain; and as the large vessels bear a very small proportion to the smaller, it is manifest that it is to the latter mainly that these very remarkable movements are to be ascribed.

We see also in the exposed brain another but much slighter movement of expansion and subsidence, corresponding to the action of the heart, which it is easy to distinguish from the slower and more extensive movements depending on respiration.

Oscillations of the hæmastatic column.—Exactly of the same significance are the oscillations of the hæmastatic column first observed by Hales. In his numerous experiments on horses and dogs, after the arterial blood had risen to its full height, he observed it rise and fall 2, 3, or 4 inches at each beat of the pulse, and then of a sudden it would fall and rise 12 or 14 inches on the animal sighing deeply or struggling. More exact observations have since shown that these more extended oscillations correspond exactly to the movements of respiration; the column falling suddenly during each inspiration, and again rising slowly during the intervals from one inspiration to another; and the extent of the fall always corresponding to the depth of the inspiration.* These oscillations take place both in the arteries and in the veins, and correspond exactly in the moment of their occurrence, like the indications of the needles of a telegraph placed far distant at the two extremities of the electric wire. No experiment could be devised more conclusive than this to show that the influence of the pneumatic force of

* Magendie, ' Phenomènes Physiques de la vie.'

the chest extends over the whole vascular system; for at the moment of inspiration the weight of the atmosphere bears down the column of blood simultaneously at the very beginning of the arteries and at the very end of the veins, thus rendering it quite certain that the same pressure takes place also at every intermediate point.

As the veins become smaller the oscillations become less extensive, just like the visible changes in the diameter of the veins. This diminution of the range of the oscillations as we recede from the heart, whether in the veins or in the arteries, has never been interpreted in its full significance; and will, hereafter, be looked to with great interest, seeing that correct theory shows the range of the oscillations in the blood-vessels at any point to be inversely as the sectional area of the blood-vessels at that point, and of course directly as the velocity of the blood in the vessel subjected to experiment.

Entrance of air into veins.—The depression of the arterial column produced by inspiration is small in relation to its total height; but the venous column near the heart is only one tenth as high as the arterial, and the depression of it from inspiration is relatively very great. It may be diminished to one half, or a quarter, or still less, and may even disappear altogether, and then the external air forcing its way into the vein would be carried with the current of blood onward to the heart, just as has been known to take place in operations in the vicinity of the cavity of the thorax in which large veins have been laid open. Great feebleness of the heart on the one hand, and, on the other, sighing or other very deep inspirations, are the causes which conspire to occasion the entrance of air into the veins; as must be obvious from considering that the former makes the hæmastatic column low, and the latter make the fall of the column great.

Asphyxia, or cessation of breathing. — Whenever the act of breathing ceases, from whatever cause, whether from submersion in water, from tying the windpipe, from obstructing the aperture of the mouth and nostrils as in suffocation or smothering, or from compressing the windpipe as in hanging or garotting—if there be a complete arrestment of the respiratory movements, a condition of the whole system is induced which terminates in death in about three and a half minutes, and may be regarded as the *experimentum crucis* of the doctrine of the pneumatic agency of the chest.

When the act of breathing ceases the heart is deprived of all assistance from the pneumatic force of the chest; it has now to contend single-handed against all the resistances which oppose the onward movement of the blood—a task for which its utmost efforts are ineffectual; it labours and palpitates in vain: the blood accumulates in the capillary vessels of the system, and more especially oppresses the brain, which it does the more readily that it is now no longer as oxygenated blood, but as black or venous blood, that it stagnates in the cerebral vessels: loss of consciousness, of sensibility, and of all other forms of nervous energy speedily ensue, and these are the fore-runners of the extinction of life.

I am aware that this doctrine of the nature of asphyxia—that it consists essentially in the inability of the heart to propel the blood through the systemic blood-vessels—is in opposition to all the explanations of it now taught in the schools of medicine; but it is a legitimate deduction from the doctrine of the pneumatic force of the chest here advocated, and must stand or fall along with it.

I may merely mention the current doctrines of the nature of asphyxia in the order of the times when they were first propounded, without entering into any critical examination of them. The doctrine of Haller was, that when the breathing ceased the heart was no longer able to propel the blood through the pulmonary blood-vessels. Goodwyn and Bichat both ascribed the death which occurs in asphyxia to unoxygenated blood, which the former regarded as no longer capable of stimulating by contact the surface of the left ventricle of the heart, while the latter held that it destroyed the irritability of the muscular substance of the heart by circulating through the coronary blood-vessels.

Dr Allison's doctrine, that the flow of blood through the pulmonary capillaries necessarily ceases, because the blood is no longer oxygenated, can only be accepted by those who believe in the influence which the act of oxygenation is supposed to exert over the progress of the blood.

Fœtal circulation. — But, it will be asked, if the respiration be necessary to carry on the circulation, how can it be performed in the fœtus in which there is no respiration? A most appropriate question crtainly, and suggestive of a very important answer. The force of the left ventricle alone may be insufficient to propel the blood through the systemic capillaries, and yet the force of both ventricles combined may be able to do so. Now, in the fœtus the two ventricles combine their strength to drive the blood through the system, and succeed in doing it. An important conclusion follows. If the same amount of force be required to carry on the systemic circulation immediately before birth in the fœtus and immediately after it in the new-born child, then the pneumatic force of the chest must be exactly equal to the force of the right ventricle of the heart; or according to the estimate deduced from Hering's experiment above cited, it must be somewhat more than one half of the force of the left ventricle.

But mathematical accuracy does not belong to physiological questions, in which we must be content with an approximative answer. It is impossible to prove that exactly the same force is required to carry on the circulation of the fœtus immediately before birth, and that through the systemic circuit of a newly born child. There are certain circumstances that might incline us to think that the former would require more force: seeing that at birth the whole length of the umbilical cord and placental vessels is subtracted from the sanguiferous circuit; the blood which occupied these vessels being now reposited in the lungs, and the right ventricle of the heart being detached to keep it in motion ; so that the left ventricle might still be equal to the duty left to it to perform. On the other hand, the whole blood of the body still requires to be propelled from the left ventricle to the right side of the heart; and it may be asked if that would not be more easily done, when a large portion of the blood flowed through the lax vessels of the placenta and the wide venous duct than when the whole of it had to be forced through the undilated capillaries of the general system, now for the first time receiving so great a tide. I incline, decidedly, to this latter opinion, which implies, that from the moment of birth the systemic circulation cannot possibly go on without the aid of the pneumatic force of the chest; unless, indeed, it happen, as in an interesting case mentioned below, that the fœtal passages being still pervious, the right ventricle is enabled to come to the rescue, and the circulation is temporarily carried on as in the fœtus by the united efforts of both ventricles.

We shall probably, therefore, not greatly err if we regard the pneumatic force of the chest at the time of birth as at least equal to the force of the right ventricle of the heart. But as life advances it becomes an agent of gradually increasing importance in carrying on the circulation of the blood. We have seen from the experiments described in last section (pp. 39—41) how effective pneumatic forces are in overcoming resistance due to the inertia of liquids. Now, the inertia of the blood depends on its weight and on the quantity of it which accumulates in the blood-vessels, more especially in the veins. This inertia is least in the fœtus and newly born child, but it gradually increases as life advances. The development of the chest and depth of the respiration keep pace with it till middle life, when the influence of the pneumatic force over the movement of the blood is highest. With advancing years, again, a more plethoric state of the veins is apt to occur, while the influence of the pneumatic force of the chest is becoming feebler and more variable, and this occasions danger to life from sudden congestion of the blood-vessels of the brain—a danger quite analogous to that which we have just described as threatening or destroying life in asphyxia. The detraction of blood seems a natural remedy in such circumstances; and this accords with the experience of the physicians of the last generation, however opposite to the inert timidity of the present race of medical men.

Transition from Fœtal to Extra-Uterine Life.—To see a child born, that is, to see it pass from the state of an aquatic animal, in which it has spent its intra-uterine life, to that of an air-breathing animal, which it assumes as soon as it comes into

the world, is one of the most striking of the many wonders
which physiology everywhere holds out to those who cultivate it.

I have always exercised all the branches of my profession,
according to the custom which was all but universal among my
contemporaries in Glasgow when I commenced medical practice
some six and forty years ago.   I cannot but regard this
custom as much superior to that which our medical corpora-
tions are now enforcing, of making every man from the beginning select for himself a single branch of the profession.   It is
true that he may in this way become practically more expert
in his own particular branch, but it is at the expense of his
general views.   He becomes like the man who makes the head
of the pin, but has no notion how it is pointed.   So it will turn
out under this new system, that the men who occupy the
highest places in the medical profession will be men of contracted ideas, like tradesmen ; and that if you wish to find a
man of large views of physiological nature, you must turn to
the more humble class of general practitioners who have learned
betimes to exercise all the branches of their art.   I do not
mean that in course of time it is not advantageous for every
man to select certain *specialties*; but that must be as taste and
reflection, and still more as opportunity and circumstances,
direct.   In my own case, my long-continued connection with
the Infirmary here, naturally turned my attention to Surgery,
and so I took to cutting for the stone,* to carving out new lips,†
and to curing strictures of the urethra by disruption,‡ a principle of treatment which I believe I first introduced into
surgical practice.   In earlier life, however, I held the office of

* " On Lithotomy, as performed with a Rectangular Staff."   Reprinted from
the ' Edinburgh Monthly Journal of Medical Science,' Feb., 1848.
   " On Lithotomy considered as a Cause of Death."   ' Glasgow Medical Journal,'
April, 1860.
   "Three Letters on Lithotomy."   'Lancet,' 1868.
   "Lithotomy in the Female."   In Dr. M'Clintock's ' Clinical Memoirs.'   Dublin,
1863.
   † " On a Method of Restoring the Lower Lip after Complete or Partial
Recision."   'London Medical Gazette,' October, 1841.   Second Edition, with
Engravings.   Glasgow, 1859.
   ‡ " Description of a Compound Catheter for the Treatment of Strictures of the
Urethra."   ' London Medical Gazette,' 1841.

district-surgeon, where my duties were almost purely medical; and I then took with my whole heart to the fever of our own city,* as I afterwards did at the Cholera Hospital to "the Malignant Cholera."† Now, it would be difficult to persuade me that I would have been a more useful man, or have better fulfilled the duties which I was destined to perform, if at the beginning of my professional career I had been starched up with an apparatus round my neck, like that which prevents the young men of the present day from ever turning round their heads out of one direction. To finish this digression. On all of the subjects above mentioned and on a few more besides, I have given to the public the results of my experience and thought, holding that to be a duty which every medical man capable of doing it owes to his profession and to those who cultivate it. Even the busiest may find time to put a few bricks in their right places in some corner of that vast Edifice —call it rather Temple, as not unworthy of a God—of which, some two thousand three hundred years ago, Hippocrates of Cos laid the foundation stone, and which ever since all genuine disciples of his have vied with each other to establish, amplify, and adorn.

These remarks are made in extenuation of the grave delict, as some will account it, of my having practised Midwifery: which I freely confess with the aggravation of having always had a pleasure in it, and that for two reasons; first, that it confers upon us the high privilege of seeing woman in her noblest and most interesting phase—at home among her children; and second, which is more pertinent to our present subject, that it supplies us with some of the most important

* "Causes and Periodical Revolutions in the Prevalence of Fever in Glasgow." In Report on Diseases of the City Poor. 'Glasgow Medical Journal,' Nov., 1830.

"Malaria considered as a Cause of Fever in Glasgow." Review of Dr M'Culloch on Malaria. 'Glasgow Medical Journal,' May, 1828.

"On the Stable Nuisance in Glasgow." 'Glasgow Medical Journal,' Oct., 1853.

† "Observations on Malignant Cholera." 'Glasgow Medical Journal,' 1833. Second Edition. London, 1848.

"On the Constitution and Distribution of the Blood in Malignant Cholera." 'Glasgow Medical Journal,' April, 1854.

facts in Physiology. I recollect once having been told boastingly by one of the only *pure* physicians we at that time had in Glasgow, that not only had he never delivered a woman of a child, which I would never have imputed to him, but, to show how immaculate he was, that he had never even been in the room when a child was born. I told him that he ought not to lose an hour in going to the Lying-in Hospital, where he would behold a sight truly worthy of being seen—one which no man of well-constituted mind, even after having seen it many times before, can again witness without fresh wonder and admiration.

The fœtus is developed under water and lives in it up to the time of birth. It has, therefore, the organization of an aquatic animal, and the transition which it has to undergo consists in modifying the aquatic organs and assuming those of an air-breathing animal.

So far as this transition can be seen externally, the most conspicuous part of it consists in a series of deep inspirations in which the whole chest is stretched to the uttermost, and this seemingly giving pain, a fit of crying is an invariable accompaniment in a vigorous infant. All this takes place in less time than I have taken to write these words, and yet a complete revolution has been effected in the internal organization which is permanent throughout after life; the circulation of the blood has been completely changed, and the continual presence within the lungs of air containing oxygen in chemical action upon the blood has become an indispensable condition of life.

The lungs of the fœtus having been developed under water and retained in the same medium till birth, the air-tubes and blood-vessels are compacted together, the elasticity of the tissues being completely overcome by the atmospheric pressure telling through the medium of the water upon the pliant walls of the chest and the parts within it, but no sooner does the child escape from the water and make a deep inspiration, than the air, having now for the first time access to the glottis, rushes into and distends the air-tubes and air-cells; the atmospheric pressure which previously told only upon the external surface is now equal without and within the lungs; and the consequence is, that the elasticity of the soft bones and cartilages of the chest and of the pulmonary tissues, which was impotent alone against the pressure of the atmosphere, comes now into play and gives a permanent superiority to the expanding forces. A quantity of air is thus introduced into the lungs which can never afterwards, so long as life continues, be expelled. It increases during inspiration and diminishes during expiration, but the utmost force of the expiratory muscles is unable to expel it.

The medium quantity of air thus introduced into the lungs, or the complement remaining after an ordinary expiration, varies according to the development of the chest in each individual. It can be most accurately measured by restoring after death the original conditions of fœtal life by extracting the air from the lungs by means of an exhausted receiver attached to the trachea; while an incision being made on each side into the cavity of the pleura, the pressure of the atmosphere tells freely on the outward surface of the lungs. In an experiment of this kind which I saw made with great care by the late Drs Jeffray and Ure of this city upon the body of an executed criminal, they found 32·6 grs. of air in the lungs, which is very nearly 109 cubic inches.

If, then, we suppose 18 cubic inches to be taken in at an ordinary inspiration, we have 127 cubic inches as the full complement of air in the lungs during tranquil respiration, and of that quantity almost exactly one seventh is interchanged at each act of respiration.

A change of the very same kind, and from the same cause, has taken place in the blood-vessels of the lungs; into which a quantity of blood has been introduced, which never can be expelled while life continues. Previous to the infant's drawing its first breath the only part of the circum-pulmonary cavity accessible to blood was that of the great veins on the right side of the heart; now it has access also to a wider space on the other side of the right ventricle, and the blood rushes in to fill the pulmonary blood-vessels. It comes in at once wherever the access is readiest. It is drawn out of the aortic system retrogressively through the arteriose duct into the expanding pulmonary arteries, while it is at the same moment forced across the auricles of the heart through the foramen ovale into the pulmonary veins. All this is done in a twinkling, and not slowly by means of the action of the heart, which probably undergoes a momentary suspension during this•great cataclysm of organic nature, and when it is at length resumed, every necessary arrangement has been made for the instauration of the new order of things. The right ventricle can never again send the blood through the arteriose duct so long as breathing continues, for at every inspiration it would be drawn backward into the pulmonary artery. The whole force of the right ventricle, therefore, is now devoted to send the blood through the pulmonary artery; and the blood with which the pulmonary capillaries are already filled being now aërated, it is forced through the pulmonary veins to the left side of the heart. Thus the new system of the circulation of the blood is established, and it is soon after rendered irreversible by the closure of the foramen ovale and the obliteration of the ductus arteriosus.

Obstetrical notes.—I conclude this sub-section with some obstetrical notes bearing upon the characters and movements of the blood, and the influence of respiration over it.

Whole blood of the fœtus black.—Some physiologists have taught that the placenta produces upon the blood the same changes as the lungs—the blood being said to be black or venous in the umbilical arteries and of a florid red colour in the umbilical vein. It is easy in cases of child-birth, by some very simple experiments, to show the inaccuracy of this opinion. If, after the child is born, instead of putting two ligatures round the cord and dividing it between them, only one ligature be applied, and after dividing the cord on the placental side of the ligature the blood be collected in a tumbler or other glass vessel, assisting the flow by stripping the cord downward, then from three to four ounces of blood can easily be obtained. Now, the blood is never partly of the one colour and partly of the other, but either wholly black or wholly red; and it can be obtained of either colour according to the mode in which the experiment is performed. If the cord be tied the moment the child draws its first breath and cries, then the whole blood, both from the arteries and from the veins, is black; but on allowing it to stand exposed to the air it becomes florid on the surface like ordinary blood, showing it to be quite susceptible of being acted on by oxygen if there had been any of that gas supplied to it by the placenta. We infer, therefore, that the black blood of the umbilical arteries undergoes no change of colour in passing through the placenta, but returns through the vein of the very same hue. If again the child be allowed to breathe freely before the cord is tied, then the whole blood obtained from the cord is of a bright red colour, which it has manifestly acquired in the lungs of the child before going to the placenta.

Do the respiratory movements ever occur before birth?—If the muscular act corresponding to inspiration were performed before birth when there is no possibility of air finding access to the lungs, it is manifest that the whole pneumatic effect would be to draw the blood from the systemic veins into the chest. Does nature ever employ this expedient to assist the circulation of the fœtus, either within the uterus or during parturition, especially when from compression of the cord or other cause the progress of the blood may be impeded? I am disposed to answer this question in the affirmative, founding my opinion on a case which occurred to me twenty-four years ago. It was a case of twins: the first of which was born easily, but not so the second, for there was an interval of no less than three hours between the births of the two children. When the lower limbs were at length brought down, there was a complete suspension of labour for half an hour, during which the child lay with its chest in the vagina, and the head still included within the uterus. As the cord was felt beating regularly and vigorously, I did not deem any interference necessary; still, however, I could not avoid satisfying myself from time to time as to the pulsation of the cord. In doing so, as my finger rested on the ribs, I was surprised to find them move, and on the movement being repeated at regular intervals, my whole attention was fully aroused, and to make my examination more sure, I placed the fingers of the other hand on the opposite side of the chest. I had then full time to satisfy myself that the ribs on both sides of the chest were undergoing alternate movements of elevation and depression, resembling exactly the rhythmic movements of respiration. All this took place at a time when, from the position of the child's head within the uterus, access of air to the mouth and nostrils was physically impossible. Strong contractions now came on, and the child was at once expelled.

Were this observation confirmed, it would be important physiologically, as evincing that the reflex acts of respiration are excited by a sense of obstruction to the passage of the blood through the heart, and not by any feeling connected with the aëration of the blood and seated in the lungs, which are dormant before birth.

I need scarcely say that the question here proposed is quite different from that which has been so much discussed, of the child actually inhaling air and crying before birth.

I may add that ever since, whenever an opportunity offered, I have carefully sought for the same phenomena, but never with success, although never with a perfect correspondence of conditions in the mother and child.

Whether any similar movements occur *in utero* might be judged of from observations made on whelps still within the transparent amnion; or just extruded and placed, before they have breathed, under water, where it is well known they can live for hours.

Twins, one of which unconsciously sucked his brother's blood, and so deprived him of life.—This case occurred fourteen years ago. I can find no memoranda made of it at the time, but the history of it was so remarkable that the essential points are as fresh in my mind as if it had taken place yesterday.

The labour on the part of the mother was easy. The child first born was remarkably vigorous, drawing up its limbs, struggling and respiring deeply. It seemed to be full-blooded, the face being tumid and somewhat livid, and the whole surface having a similar hue. It cried lustily before the cord was tied, and there was no unusual delay in tying it. The other child presented a marked contrast to the first. It was pale and exsanguine. It lay fully extended, and never bent a limb, although its joints were quite flexible. It never cried, but after some time a feeble respiration was established. I could not view these appearances without much alarm, and unfortunately the idea of hæmorrhage from the placenta presented itself to my mind, and I immediately tied the cord which was still beating, much to my regret on reflection afterwards. The child was kept warm, and was able to take a little nourishment. It continued to breathe feebly, and survived about thirty hours. I may add, that I never saw a more beautiful child than this; its pure white skin resembling Parian marble, and its perfect symmetry coming fully out as it lay straight and with extended limbs, an attitude in which a living child is so rarely seen.

There was only one oval placenta to which both cords were attached. I brought it away with me, and gave it to Professor Allen Thompson, who kindly undertook to examine it. He found free vascular communication throughout every part of it, so that a liquid injected through the vessels of the one umbilical cord returned readily by the other.

It is clear from this history that the child first born, by the vigorous inspirations made during his prolonged fit of crying, filled his own vessels, both pulmonary and systemic, with blood, and so unconsciously drained off from the placenta the share of the vital fluid which should have been the heritage of his brother.

Could the circumstances have been foreseen, the cord of the child first born should have been tied without a moment's delay, so as to prevent any undue draining of the placental veins; while the tying of the cord of the second child should have been deferred as long as possible, that is, till after the expulsion of the placenta, which should have been compressed, and the cord stripped downward towards the child.

Whenever, therefore, a child is weak from want of blood, the greater the delay in tying the cord so much the better for the child; because the umbilical arteries contracting under the influence of the cold, and meeting with a greater resistance

6

from the gradual coagulation of the blood in the capillaries of the placenta, are continually sending less blood thereto, while the aspirations of the child through the umbilical veins are continually becoming stronger under the influence of the oxygenated blood, and the whole difference between the blood sent to the placenta and that drawn from it tells in favour of the child. Besides which the compression of the placenta after extrusion, and the stripping of the cord downward towards the child, give an additional supply of blood, which is the great requirement.

Repeated alternations, after birth, of the fœtal and adult circulations, corresponding to periods of apnœa and respiration.—This case occurred somewhat more than thirty years ago. I transcribe it from my note-book with the title under which it is there inserted, and only leaving out an expression of opinion which I have long since believed to be erroneous.

CASE OF CONGENITAL DEFICIENCY IN THE ŒSOPHAGUS

The following case is one of great interest, both on account of the very remarkable symptoms which it presented, and the uncommon malformation in which it originated. The infant, which was a male, was born about the eighth month. It cried, but not lustily, on coming into the world, and though small it seemed perfectly well formed in all its members. In about half an hour afterwards, when I first examined it carefully, there was a good deal of phlegm in its throat, which occasioned a difficulty in breathing, but the phlegm was at length got up, and the breathing became natural. Everything went on well till the nurse gave it some sugar and water, which brought on a violent fit of suffocation, attended with lividity all over the body. These fits occurred afterwards on every attempt to make the child swallow. There was great difficulty of breathing, with a rattling noise in the throat, and relief was never obtained without a discharge of frothy fluid from the mouth and nose, to promote which the nurse held the child inclined forward with its head depending. But the most remarkable circumstance attending these fits was that in some of the more violent the respiration at length ceased altogether, and continued suspended during a period of about five minutes or more, when the face and whole surface of the body became perfectly livid. The pulse, however, instead of ceasing along with the suspended breathing, became fuller, and stronger than before, clearly showing that the blood was taking the course observed in the fœtal state, and not passing through the lungs. The increase of the strength and fulness of the pulse probably arose from the combined impulse of both ventricles being greater than that of the left ventricle alone. This was observed twice by myself and once by my friend, Dr James Watson,—now the venerable father of the medical faculty in Glasgow,—whom I consulted upon the case. On introducing an elastic catheter into the œsophagus it stopped always at the same point, and on inject-ing some milk down through it an immediate regurgitation took place, through the nose and mouth. All attempts to give nourishment by the mouth were therefore abandoned during the second day, and although it was clear that the child could not live, it had nutrient enemata from time to time, which, however, had probably little effect in protracting its sufferings. It died fifty-four hours after birth.

On examining the body the œsophagus was found to termi-nate in a shut sac a little below the bifurcation of the trachea. The tunics of the canal were quite perfect as far as the point, where they terminated abruptly, as was distinctly felt on com-pressing them between the finger and thumb. No trace of muscular fibres could be discovered further down, accompany-ing the plexus of the par vagum in the posterior mediastinum; but exactly at the diaphragm the œsophagus recommenced. On opening the stomach the œsophagus was found to enter it in the usual way at the cardiac orifice and to extend as high as the diaphragm, where it terminated abruptly in a cul-de-sac. There was thus a space of about an inch and a half where the œsophagus was completely awanting. The child in every other respect was perfectly formed. The stomach, bowels, and other abdominal viscera were healthy, and the distribution of the great vessels and nerves was normal.

The heart was distended with blood, and the ductus

arteriosus full. The foramen ovale appeared to me on my first examination to be quite open, as I saw through it from the right into the left auricle of the heart, but on subsequently opening the left side of the heart also it was found that the foramen ovale was completely closed by a very thin diaphanous membrane, which had not till then been distinguishable. The membrane, though very thin, was nevertheless entire, so that no blood could pass directly from the one auricle of the heart to the other without rupturing it. From this it is obvious that the membrane must have been organized during the last thirty hours of life, or subsequently to the last attempt to give milk by the mouth, when the fœtal circulation was re-established for the last time.

The fits of suffocation in this case were obviously brought on by the fluid swallowed being stopped at the upper cul-de-sac of the œsophagus, and in consequence regurgitating, and in part entering the larynx, causing spasmodic closure of the glottis. During the fits of suffocation the fœtal circulation re-established itself, as was obvious from the colour of the skin and the state of the pulse, as well as from the great length of time during which the respiration was completely suspended without the extinction of life. On the fluid being discharged at the mouth and nose by inclining the child forward with the head depending, the spasm of the glottis ceased, and respiration re-commenced by sobbing and crying as in the new-born infant, when the circulation of the adult was again established. The death seemed to be altogether the effect of exhaustion and not of any fit of suffocation.

To the preceding history, written three and thirty years ago, and the remarks unbiassed by any theory then made upon it, I shall merely add a single observation as to the two paths which the blood may pursue in the newly born child, in which the fœtal passages, by the foramen ovale and arteriose duct, are still patent. If the respiration is going on the fœtal circulation is impossible, and the whole force of the right ventricle is devoted to the pulmonary circulation, so as to keep the pulmonary blood-vessels always full; for without that, at every inspiration, a portion of the blood of the aorta would be forced backward by the atmospheric pressure through the arteriose duct. If again the respiration be suspended in the newly born child the fœtal circulation is restored, as repeatedly occurred in the preceding case; and we have then the whole force of the left ventricle, and the best part of the force of the right directed to propel the blood over the general system, and only a small portion of the latter employed in keeping up an imperfect circulation through the lungs.

II.—*Pneumatic Phenomena of Indefinite Origin*

The phenomena of this class are probably not referrible to any single cause; and may originate from the action of the heart, or of the pleurocardiac apparatus described above. They are best distinguished negatively by the want of those alternations of intensity and relaxation corresponding to the respiratory movements which belong to the phenomena we have just been considering.

They are confined chiefly to the veins, and capillary vessels, which are in a state quite different from that which they would assume if the blood were propelled through them solely by the force of the heart; while they are exactly in the state which they would assume if the blood moved under the influence of two forces, the one propelling it from behind, while the other draws it onward by aspiration towards the centre of the circulating system.

Without pretending to analyse and enumerate the phenomena of this class, I shall merely select and describe two of them as illustrations of their general nature.

If, according to the former of the two suppositions stated above, the blood were propelled solely by the force of the heart, then it is manifest that the veins and capillary vessels would be in a state of constant distension; for the same force which propelled the blood forward along the axis of the vessels would press it also laterally against their coats, and so keep them in a state of turgescence. Further, all vessels equidistant from the heart would exhibit the same degree of turgescence; and the more distant the vessels were from the end of the circuit, that is, from the right side of the heart, their turgescence would, *cæteris paribus*, be the greater.

But how different is the actual state of these vessels! The veins appear, for the most part, to be only half filled. It is only when the blood is prevented from flowing freely towards the heart that they become turgid. The compression of a single vein produces no change upon it, as the blood passes unimpeded by collateral channels. It is only when the whole collateral channels are also obstructed, as by a ligature round the limb, that the blood accumulates in the veins and capillaries and renders them turgid.

The phenomena of venous hæmorrhage lead to the same conclusion, or rather present the same argument in different terms. If the heart were the sole moving power, the turgid veins, when wounded, would bleed profusely; the tendency of the blood to issue laterally being greater than its tendency to follow the axis of the wounded vein, for in the former direction it spouts out unopposed, while in the latter it is opposed by the whole column of blood which it has to push onward to the right side of the heart. But how different are the phenomena as they actually present themselves! The flow of blood from a wounded vein generally ceases spontaneously. We have never any trouble in arresting it unless the vein be of such a size, or so situated, that the blood which it carries cannot easily and readily be transmitted by some of the numerous collateral channels, for which the venous system is so conspicuous. Now this is exactly what would take place on the hypothesis of two forces, for the blood issuing through a wound would be opposed by the pressure of the atmosphere, while it would be, as it were, solicited by the central pneumatic forces to pass along the axis of the vein, or if that were obstructed, through some collateral channel.

To make a wounded vein bleed, we are compelled to have recourse to artificial expedients, as in performing venesection, when we bind a ribbon round the arm between the heart and the wound. We thus completely destroy the influence of the pneumatic forces which are opposed to the flow of blood, and allow the propulsive force which is in favour of it to act alone.

SECTION IV.—*History of Opinions as to the Influence of Pneumatic Forces on the Circulation of the Blood*

Haller was well acquainted with the influence which the act of inspiration exercises upon the movement of the blood in the great veins near the thorax. Much of the description given above is in his words, or in words of similar import. He, however, regarded the act of respiration not as promoting the circulation of the blood, but merely as modifying it, since he believed the effects of expiration to be just the reverse of those of inspiration. He explained the movement of the blood produced by inspiration on the principle of derivation—*vis derivationis*. This, it might be argued, includes the principle of pneumatic force; but Haller certainly did not use the term in that precise sense when he illustrates the nature of derivation, by saying that when a blood-vessel is opened all the neighbouring parts send supplies towards the aperture—*qua, data porta, ruunt.*

To Dr Carson of Liverpool, unquestionably, belongs the credit of being the author of the doctrine of the indispensable necessity of a pneumatic force to carry on the circulation of the blood. During his whole lifetime, indeed, he was zealously occupied in promulgating and defending this doctrine. When he graduated at the University of Edinburgh in the year 1799, he published an inaugural thesis on the subject. This was followed in 1815 by a more formal treatise, of which he published in 1833 an enlarged edition, containing many new arguments and a spirited reply to Dr Arnott and his other antagonists. He believed the pneumatic force to be seated solely in the heart. He rejects the rival views of Sir David Barry as to a pneumatic force seated in the thorax. We owe to him some important observations as to the influence of the elasticity of the lungs which, had he analysed them more accurately, would certainly have led him to a clear knowledge of the pneumatic doctrine; but he very unaccountably restricts the influence of the elasticity of the lungs to the heart alone. Dr Carson also refers to the elasticity of the lungs, the immediate occurrence of the act of expiration on the relaxation of the inspiratory muscles. It certainly concurs with the elasticity of the costal cartilages and the gravity of the parts displaced by inspiration to bring on the act of expiration in a purely physical way.

Sir David Barry, on the contrary, adopts the doctrine of a pneumatic force seated in the thorax, while he denies the existence of any similar power seated in the heart. From the account he gives of the pneumatic force of the thorax, it is obvious that he regarded it as very similar to the force of a common syringe, and that he makes no account of the delicate complication of forces which results from the simultaneous entrance of air and of a liquid into the same expanding cavity. But the great glory of Sir David is his having instituted experiments upon live animals to prove the existence of the pneumatic force of the chest. With respect to the experiments in which he introduced a tube filled with a coloured liquid through an aperture in the throracic parietes into the cavities of the pleura and pericardium respectively, while the lower end of the tube was immersed in the liquid, it cannot, I think, be doubted that such an experiment would succed, and the liquid accumulate in the cavities, just as is stated to have taken place. As to the experiment, again, in which he introduced a tube in the same way into the jugular vein, it is difficult to see how the liquid should have flowed inward, and why, on the contrary, the blood did not flow outward through the tube; since it is precisely in that way, only turning the tube upward, that we measure the hæmastatic column which Hales found to stand in the jugular vein of the horse at the height of 12 inches. It is possible, however, when from exhaustion of strength the column fell very low, that the liquid might flow into the vein just as the external air rushes into it in similar circumstances. It might happen also from the pressure of the ligatures binding the animal upon the other veins entering the chest. I can see no reason, therefore, to join with Dr Arnott in discrediting Barry's experiments, and the high authorities by which they are supported.

Magendie had a firm belief in the pneumatic force both of the chest and of the heart. His experiments made in conjunction with M. Poiseuille are of the highest importance, and can never lose their value to physiology, whatever interpretation be put upon them ; but certainly, as interpreted by Magendie himself, they do not remove the difficulties or reconcile the alleged inconsistencies of the pneumatic theory. He repeats continually that the chest is neither more nor less than a common pump, but he takes no notice of the manifest difference between them, inasmuch as the chest is destitute of valves which are an indispensable part of the mechanism of a common pump. According to his view, as stated with perfect frankness, the action of the chest is to draw in the venous blood when the ribs are elevated, and to force it out again when the ribs are depressed. He seems to suffer no embarrassment from reflecting that it is difficult to see how the circulation can be expedited by these alternate but opposite movements. Haller held exactly the same opinion, but that cautious reasoner ranks the respiration among the causes which modify and not as one of those which promote the circulation of the blood. The error which underlies the whole of Magendie's doctrine is his belief that the effect of expiration is to force the blood back from the chest into the veins. In the beautiful experiments made with the hæmadynamometer to illustrate the influence of respiration on the height of the mercurial column, he invariably refers the rise of the mercury during expiration to the blood being forced backward by the compression of the chest. It seems never to have occurred to him that the phenomenon might be due to the afflux of blood from behind rather than to the reflux of it from before. In like manner he held that the influence of inspiration extended only to a limited distance from the chest along the venous system, instead of regarding it as due to the atmospheric pressure everywhere telling upon the blood-vessels, both veins and arteries, and forcing the blood through them in the direction where the resistance is least. The chest certainly resembles a common pump in so

far as inspiration is concerned; but here the parallel stops :
the common pump is provided with a valve at its inlet which
prevents it from forcing the liquid backward. In the chest
there is no such valve, but, notwithstanding, the blood is not
forced backward. This is provided for by a totally different
mechanism, which has been explained above as constituting the
essential peculiarity in the structure of the "respiratory
pump." In virtue of this mechanism, the blood once within
the chest is sheltered from all compression, and has therefore
no tendency to flow backward, but accumulates quietly, as in
a reservoir, for the supply of the heart. Magendie seems to
have relied altogether on his experiments, as attested by the
evidence of his senses, without troubling his head about theoretical objections. Thus he takes no notice of the writings of
Dr Arnott, although he was, without question, acquainted with
them, seeing that he joins in raising the cry of " physiquement
impossible " against Sir David Barry, for what reason it is
difficult to discover, the opinions of Barry being so nearly
identical with his own,—at least, in so far as the chest is concerned, while they differ as to the pneumatic force of the heart
which was recognised by Magendie.

The late Professor Jeffrey, of our own University, was a
strenuous advocate for the sucking power of the heart. He
was a follower of Carson, and so far as I recollect did not
recognise any pneumatic force seated in the thorax. It is to
be regretted that his lectures upon this subject, which seemed
to be carefully written out, but unfortunately, as I have since
been told by his son, unintelligible from being written in
shorthand, have never been made public. They certainly produced a powerful impression upon the juvenile auditory to
which they were addressed, and made many converts among
them, of whom I was one. Not many years afterwards
Dr Arnott's thundering denunciation of the whole doctrine
appeared in the second edition of his elements of natural
philosophy, and was generally believed to have struck it down
for ever. I did not see the work for many years afterwards,
but having at the time read an account of it, with extracts in
the 'Edinburgh Medical and Surgical Journal,' and feeling

indignant at the author's dogmatism and his unworthy treatment of his opponents and of the whole medical profession, I
wrote a criticism on Dr Arnott's views, exposing in particular
the fallacy of his "bloodless experiment," and his unfairness
in ascribing to Dr Barry opinions he did not entertain for the
purpose of refuting them. This criticism was never published,
but on lately searching out the old manuscript I was pleased
to find it in perfect accordance with the views stated above.
Ever since my appointment, in the year 1839, to the Chair
of Physiology in the University of Glasgow, I have publicly
taught the doctrine of the pneumatic force both of the chest
and of the heart, but it was only during the summer of last
year (1868) that I found time to examine minutely the principles on which it rests.

APPENDIX

ON THE

ESTIMATE MADE BY REV. DR HAUGHTON

OF THE

FORCE OF THE HUMAN HEART

(' *Lancet*,' *November* 12, 1870.)

As the force of the human heart is a subject that can never lose its interest to physiologists, I desire to submit the following observations upon it, suggested by an estimate of it recently made by the Rev. Dr Haughton, of which an account is contained in the 'Dublin Quarterly Journal of Medical Science,' vol. xlix, p. 47, under the title " On the Mechanical Work done by the Human Heart." I merely premise that I wish to speak of the reverend gentleman with the most perfect respect, and that I am not the less indebted to him for his testimony on behalf of my opinions that it has been unintentionally and, indeed, unconsciously given.

I shall first endeavour to show that the solution of the problem of the heart's action proposed by Dr Haughton is, so far as it goes, essentially the same as that which I laid before the profession nearly two years ago. I shall next endeavour to show that Dr Haughton's solution, although capable of determining the mechanical equivalent of the work done by the heart, cannot be employed to determine more minutely the work which the heart actually performs, and gives us erroneous ideas when we attempt so to employ it.

Let it, in the first instance, be taken for granted that there is no error in the data on which our respective computations are based, so that we may have nothing to consider but the use which is made of them.

The three elements which Dr Haughton assumes as the groundwork of his computation are, that the heart contracts 75 times in a minute; that at each contraction the left ventricle of the heart discharges three ounces of blood; and that the hæmastatic column in man stands at a height of 9·923 feet. He now multiplies the quantity of blood discharged at each contraction by the height of the hæmastatic column (3 × 9·923 =29·769) and regards the product as indicating the number of ounces that are raised one foot by each contraction of the heart. He again multiplies the product by the number of contractions of the heart in twenty-four hours, and so he obtains 89·706 foot-tons as the measure of the daily work done by the left ventricle of the heart.

In addition to Dr Haughton's three elements, I avail myself of a fourth—viz., the area of the ventricular orifice of the aorta,* which I estimate with Kiel as equal to ·4187 of a square inch, and which I regard as an element of the very highest importance in the solution of the problem of the heart's action, and the more so that it can be determined with ease, and is therefore more worthy of reliance than are some of the other elements.

Supposing, then, that we add the element just mentioned to Dr Haughton's other three, the following is the mode in which I employ these elements to determine the force of the heart. The weight of a cylinder of blood 9·923 feet in height, and having a base of ·4187 of an inch, is 30·20838 ounces. Three ounces of blood, which the heart discharges at each contraction, fill of such a cylinder 11·8245 inches, or ·985375 of a foot. Now, multiplying together the two numbers thus found, I obtain a product of 29·769, the identical result obtained by Dr Haughton—

$$30·208 \times ·985375 = 3 \times 9·923 = 29·769.$$

* See note, p. 6.

I had therefore reason in saying that Dr Haughton's computation is essentially the same as mine, seeing that their results are identical.

The same coincidence holds with respect to my own computation, and comes out still more strikingly owing to the greater simplicity of the numbers. I assume that the heart beats 72 times in a minute, that it discharges two ounces of blood at each contraction, and that the height of the hæmastatic column in man is 88 inches. Now, the weight of a cylinder of blood 88 inches in height, and having a basis of ·4187 of a square inch, is 22 ounces. Further, two ounces of blood, the quantity discharged at each contraction, fill exactly, of such a cylinder, 8 inches. Dr Haughton's computation is 2×88, and that is exactly equivalent to my computation, 22×8; the common product being 176, which denotes the number of ounces which are lifted one inch at each contraction, and by dividing 176 by 12 we obtain the number of ounces that are lifted one foot— viz., 14·66. Dr Haughton's number for each contraction is more than double, 29·769; but in addition he makes the heart beat 75 times in a minute, instead of 72 times, so that his total estimate of the day's work is to mine in the proportion of 30·774 to 14·66. But this difference does not depend on any difference in our modes of computation, which lead exactly to the same result, but merely on the different magnitudes assumed of the elements which form the base of the computations.

Neither are these accidental coincidences; for it is easy to show that the numbers obtained by Dr Haughton's method are necessarily the same as those obtained by mine. For let W denote the weight of a cylinder of blood having a base of ·4187 of an inch, and a height (H) equal to that of the hæmastatic column, and let h be the portion of that cylinder equal in volume to the blood emitted from the heart at each contraction, while w denotes the weight of the same quantity of blood. Then, as the weights of any two portions of the same liquid are as their volumes, we have—

$$w : W :: h : H; \text{ and consequently}$$
$$wH = Wh.$$

Now, Dr Haughton's method consists in calculating wH, and mine consists in calculating Wh, quantities which are necessarily equal, so that the two methods must in all cases lead to the same result.

I have thus shown that the solution of the problem of the heart's action proposed by Dr Haughton is, so far as it goes, essentially and necessarily the same as that which I laid before the profession nearly two years ago, and I now proceed to show that Dr Haughton's solution, although capable of determining accurately the mechanical equivalent of the work done by the heart, cannot be employed to determine more minutely the work which the heart actually performs, and misleads us when we attempt so to employ it.

To determine the work actually performed by the heart is a problem quite different from that of determining the mechanical equivalent of the work done. The very same effective force is required to raise one pound to a height of ten feet, as to raise ten pounds to a height of one foot, or five pounds to a height of two feet, or two pounds to a height of five feet. In all of these cases, and others innumerable if we descend to fractional numbers, the mechanical equivalent is the same, or ten foot-pounds; but the operations themselves are very different, and with respect to any organ acting in the living body, or any inanimate machine, we would not rest satisfied till we knew which was the operation it actually performed. Now it is just so with respect to the heart. There are questions in physiology as Dr Haughton has shown, to answer which the mechanical equivalent of the heart's action, or the total amount of its effective force, is all that we require to know. But there are other and more important questions for which that meagre knowledge is insufficient. The physiologist wishes to know, not only the amount of the effective force of the heart, but also in what precise way or ways that force is expended within the body. What is wanted will be better understood when I say that the effective force of the heart communicates to the blood its momentum, and that the momentum of the blood is expressed by $(q \times v)$ the mass of blood which is set in motion multiplied by the velocity with which it moves. Now we should at once attain our end if we could determine the respective values of q and v. But it is just because we cannot do so directly that we are obliged to have recourse to empirical formulæ. But such formulæ are only valuable as they agree, term to term, with the rational formula $(q \times v)$. Now Dr Haughton's formula $(w \times H)$ and mine $(W \times h)$ cannot both agree, seeing that the terms are inverted—that which expresses the mass moved in the one, expressing the velocity in the other. We must judge, therefore, which of these formulæ gives the most probable view of the moving mass and velocity of the blood. Taking Dr Haughton's data, and viewing them in the light of his own formula (wH), we have 3 ounces of blood moved over 9·923 feet at each beat of the heart, or with an initial velocity of very nearly 750 feet per minute; which is manifestly a *reductio ad absurdum*. But if to the same data we apply the formula (Wh), we invert the ratio of the mass to the velocity, and find 30·2 oz. of blood moving over ·985 of a foot at each beat of the heart, or with an initial velocity of 73·875 feet in the minute; which, though a high rate, is no longer so extravagant as to be incredible.

In conclusion, I may be allowed to say that I am still inclined to think favorably of my own more moderate estimate—that the heart at each contraction exerts a force which would be in equilibrium if counterbalanced by a weight of 22 oz. + 129·28 grs. The mode in which this force is expended is most easily explained by supposing that we have a tube 88 inches in height and ·4187 of an inch in base, that this tube is exactly filled with blood, and that at each contraction of the heart 2 additional ounces are forced into it at the lower end, lifting the whole column over a space of 8 inches, and causing an equal overflow at the top. This represents accurately the labour of the human heart, and supplies us with two numbers to express it; the one, 22 oz., being the weight of the column of blood; and the other, 8 inches, the space over which the column is lifted. The former of these numbers denotes the resistance that has to be overcome in forcing two ounces of blood into the aorta, and pushing before it the whole mass of blood in the blood-vessels; the latter, again, denotes the velocity with which the blood issues from the heart. Multiplying these two numbers together, we obtain the momentum which the heart communicates to the blood— 22 oz. moving with a velocity of 8 inches during the period of a pulsation, or of 10 inches per second, or 50 feet per minute. This is equivalent to 176 oz. (22×8) lifted 1 inch, or 14·66 oz. lifted 1 foot, during the period of a pulsation; or of 65·9 foot-pounds in a minute, or 42·3 foot-tons in twenty-four hours.

P.S.—The facility with which the force of the heart, in whatever aspect we choose to contemplate it, can be obtained from the weights and volumes of the columns of blood A, B, C, which have severally a basis of ·4187 of an inch, seems to me to show well the importance of assuming the area of the ventricular orifice of the aorta* as an element in computing the force of the heart.

A is the calculated hæmastatical column.

B is the observed hæmastatical column.

C is a column equal in volume to the capacity of the left ventricle of the heart.

	Weight in oz. av.		Volume, as height of column, in inches.
$A =$	22·301	......	89·165797
$B =$	22·	......	88·
$C =$	2·	......	8·

Force of Heart.

1. Statical equivalent $= A = 22·$ oz. $+ 129·28$ grs.
2. Dynamical equivalent $= B \times C$, the weight of the one into the volume of the other.

$$\left.\begin{array}{c} 22 \times 8· \\ 2 \times 88· \end{array}\right\} = 176 \text{ inch ounces} = 14\frac{3}{4} \text{ foot-ounces.}$$

3. Momentum of blood as emitted from heart,
   $=$ weight $B \times$ volume $C = 22$ oz. moved over a space of 8 inches at each pulsation; or with a velocity of 10 inches per second.

* See note, p. 6.

7

WRITINGS OF THE AUTHOR

AND OF THE LATE

DR. A. B. BUCHANAN,

CHIEFLY ON

PHYSIOLOGY, OR ON MEDICINE AND SURGERY.

TEMPUS EST ABEUNDI: SARCINAS COLLIGE.

PHYSIOLOGY.

1. Remarks on Phrenology.—*Anderson's Quarterly Journal of the Medical Sciences, January,* 1825.

BLOOD — PROPERTIES AND REACTIONS OF, PARTICULARLY ITS COAGULATION.

2. Contributions to the Physiology and Pathology of the Animal Fluids.—*London Medical Gazette, 9th, 16th, and 23rd April,* 1836.
3. On the White or Opaque Serum of the Blood.—*Proceedings of the Glasgow Philosophical Society, March,* 1844.
4. Farther Observations on the State of the Blood after taking Food. —*Ib., March,* 1845.
5. On the Fibrin contained in the Animal Fluids, the mode in which it Coagulates, and the Transformations it undergoes.—*Ib.,* 1844.
6. On the Coagulation of the Blood, and other Fibriniferous Liquids. —*Ib., February,* 1845.
7. Case of White Fibro-Serous Discharge from the Thigh.—*London Medico-Chirurgical Transactions,* 1863.
8. Physiological Effects of the Inhalation of Ether.—*Proceedings of the Glasgow Philosophical Society, February,* 1847.
9. On the Wound of the Ferret, with Observations on the Instincts of Animals.—*Ib.,* Volume II.
10. Darlingism, misnamed Electro-Biology.—*Glasgow,* 1862.
11. Mechanical Theory of the Predominance of the Right Hand over the Left, or more generally of the Muscles of the Right side over those of the Left side of the Body.—*Glasgow,* 1862.

12. Dr. Scouler's Account of Aristotle's Views on the same Subject.—*Proceedings of the Glasgow Philosophical Society*, 1862.
13. Theory of the Right Hand.—*Edinburgh Medical Journal*, 1863.
14. Classification of the Functions of the Human Body, and the Principles on which it Rests.—*London*, 1867.
15. On the Forces which carry on the Circulation of the Blood.—*Glasgow*, 1869-70.

MEDICINE AND SURGERY.

16. Dupuytren's, singular case of Trepan.—*Quarterly Journal of Foreign and British Medicine and Surgery, April*, 1823.
17. Malaria—Review of Dr. M'Culloch's Work on that Subject.—*Glasgow Medical Journal, May*, 1828.
18. Case of Ascites, in which the Abdomen was tapped through the Fundus of the Bladder.—*Ib., May*, 1828.
19. On the Diagnostic Symptoms of Dislocation of the Femur into the Ischiatic Notch.—*Ib.*, 1828.
20. Additional Note on the same Subject, with an Engraving.—*Ib.*, 1828.
21. Observations on the Evidence of Dr. John Thomson, of Edinburgh, in a case of Gunshot Wound.—*Glasgow Medical Journal, February*, 1830.
22. Synoptical View of Inflammatory Affections of the Surface of the Body.—*Ib., February*, 1830.
23. The Theory and Classification of Inflammations of the Skin.—*Edinburgh Medical Journal*, 1863.
24. Report of Diseases prevalent among the Poor of Glasgow during the Summer of 1830.—*Glasgow Medical Journal, November*, 1830.
25. Mode in which Cysts are formed in the Urinary Bladder.—*Ib., May*, 1830.
26. Observations on Malignant Cholera.—*Ib., April*, 1833.—*Second Edition, London*, 1848.
27. On the Constitution and Distribution of the Blood in Malignant Cholera.—*Glasgow Medical Journal, April*, 1854.
28. On a remarkable Cure of an Open Cancer of the Mamma.—*London Medical Gazette*, 1836.
29. On the Physiological and Therapeutical Effects of Iodine, given in very large doses in the forms of Iodide of Starch. Hydriodic Acid, and Iodide of Potassium.—*Ib.*, 1835-36, *and* 1836-37.
30. Fatal Cases of Obstruction and Enormous Distention of the Belly, arising from a peculiar Conformation of the Colon.—*Ib., July and August*, 1839.

31. Description of a Compound Catheter for the Treatment of Strictures of the Urethra.—*London Medical Gazette*, 1841.
32. On the Cure of Strictures of the Urethra by Disruption. Comparison of the Compound Catheter with Mr. Wakeley's Stricture Instrument.—*Lancet, March*, 1858.
33. On a Method of Restoring the Lower Lip after complete or partial Recision.—*Ib.*, 1841.—*Second Edition, with Engravings.* Glasgow, 1859.
34. Case of Suppuration in the Maxillary Sinus treated by Insufflation.—*Edinburgh and London Medical Journal*, 1843.
35. On Lithotomy as performed with a Rectangular Staff.—*Reprinted from the Edinburgh Monthly Medical Journal, February*, 1848.
36. Taille Medio-Laterale Sous-Bulbeuse.—*Paris*, 1860.
37. On Lithotomy considered as a Cause of Death.—*Glasgow Medical Journal, April*, 1860.
38. Three Letters on Lithotomy.—*Lancet*, 1868.
39. Observations on Malignant Cholera.—*Glasgow Medical Journal*, 1833.—*Second Edition. London*, 1848.
40. On the Constitution and Distribution of the Blood in Malignant Cholera.—*Glasgow Medical Journal, April*, 1854.
41. On the Stable Nuisance in Glasgow.—*Ib.*, 1853.
42. Case of Malignant Fibro-Cellular Tumor involving the Ileum.—*Ib.*, April, 1854.

43. Of Monopolies in Learning, with Remarks on the present state of Medical Education.—*Glasgow*, 1834.
44. Death of Mr. Candlish (Brother to the Very Rev. Principal Candlish, Free Church College, Edinburgh).—*Glasgow Medical Journal, March*, 1829.
45. Motion, at a Meeting of the Senate of the University of Glasgow, to confer the Degree of LL.D. on Mr. Livingstone (now of world-wide reputation, then unknown by name to any member of Senate but the mover).—1847.
46. Degrees in Science—Amendment on Motion to confer Degrees under the title of "Degrees in Natural Science."—1867.

PRINTED BY J. E. ADLARD, BARTHOLOMEW CLOSE.

www.ingramcontent.com/pod-product-compliance
Lightning Source LLC
Chambersburg PA
CBHW032147010726
47493CB00008BA/2619